Praise for *Type N*

"Can you imagine being the CURE ALL for all types of disease and problems? Can you imagine going from the NOBODY, that every one over looks and forgets is there, to the major SOMEBODY that no one will leave alone? If you want a book that's: fast paced, starts off right from page one in to the thick of things, a twist, betrayal, murder, quick resolution, holds your attention from the get go, and a little romance thrown in to a unique story, then look no further."
　　　　　—Jenn Morgan, leader of New Adult Corner Book Club

"This book takes you on a fast-paced, exciting adventure with a cast of characters that you instantly connect with. I love, love, love the story line, the twists and turns zoom along from page to page. This book got my heart beating fast, made me laugh out loud, and gave me a day of refreshing delight as I lay in my hammock on a hot summer day reading it in one sitting! I wonder if the author will bless us with another sequel or two. Get this book!"
　　　　　—Kay Henry

"*Type N* is a gripping read with the perfect ending."
　　　　　—Kira Watson, blogger of My Dear Bibliophage

"Well-crafted and exquisitely written, *Type N* is definitely a page turner. From the first page to the last, Michelle had me hooked to the story with grips of steel. This book receives five stars from me for getting my attention and never letting go. It opened my eyes to the many possibilities in this world. The intricate layers composed of faith and fate add to the equanimity of this novel. From religious readers to fiction lovers, this book is a must-read for everyone. I highly recommend this book!"
　　　　　—Harold Ekeh

"Wow. Just wow. I loved this book. Absolutely love this book. This first read book made me see a whole new side to the world... Michelle N. Onuorah puts you in a speeding jet that goes into a tailspin and crashing to earth…You will never see the government the same again. This novel truly is an example of human nature and the will to survive…This book gets straight to the point and never slows down. You will be hooked from the first page, so be ready for the ride."

—Danielle Wilson

"If you enjoy the writing styles of Stephanie Meyers or Orson Scott Card I highly recommend *Type N*. Ms. Onuorah skillfully engages her readers by introducing you to a relatable protagonist that has been blessed or cursed with an incredible world changing ability. She deftly and honestly engages moral ethical struggles, burgeoning theology, and a blossoming relationship that leaves the reader wishing for more. Her character development is much appreciated in a time where authors seem to care more about flash and dazzle then substance. The only criticism I have is that I wish there was more. I definitely see this book easily adaptable to film because the dialogue, character development, and story are already served up!"

—Micah Lemon

"While reading, I could feel the tension between characters and connected with the protagonist right away. Without giving too much away, there was one part that had me pacing the room worried about the characters. The book isn't all action, there is some good relief that will make you smile and laugh…"

—Dannica June Anderson

"A must read - it needs to be made into a movie! There is action and romance and it's just a really awesome story! The book was so much on my mind that I dreamed of Nikki and Jason all morning! Got up at nine and finished it quickly!"

—Lisa (Moon) White

"I don't give 5's often but I was impressed by this novel. A solid story that moved quickly but you were able to follow right along."

—Daniel Ace

"*Type N* was the best way I could have started my summer reading list. Fast-paced, captivating, and thought-provoking, this short novel isn't one I could put down! Also, I can be a critic when it comes to literature that incorporates faith, but this book will not disappoint. *Type N* left me wanting more!"

—Charity Thatcher

"A book [has] to grab me from the first word to the last to receive five stars. This book achieved this."

—Amazon Reviewer

"There's not a dull moment throughout the book. I could not put it down. A great read for young or old."

—Amazon Reviewer

"I was hooked from the first page and read it in one sitting."

—Amazon Reviewer

"This book has everything: action, humor, romance and faith, with a dash of mystery tied in. I love the unique storyline and how well it is developed throughout the book. With its twists, turns, and intriguing plot, *Type N* falls into the category of books that takes hostage your attention and keeps the pages turning until the very end. I would love to see this novel hitting the production studios and being made into film one day. I tip my hat to the author for a work well-done."

—Irma Costantino

"Well, well, well…WHAT a book! My heart was pounding the entire time I read this book; it was like a giant thrill ride that never ends. I love how within all this sadness and fear, there is humor and love, just the right amount to alleviate the tension in the atmosphere. This is probably one of the most unique and interesting story plots I have read for a long time. I chose to read it not because of the romance factor but for the creative, action-packed plot it had. And when I say creative, it has action, mystery, betrayal, political scandal, and romance. This is one that has it all!"

—"Lady Vigilante," Goodreads reader

"I read this book in one day because it was so compelling. It's a great story idea, and I think it contains timely and insightful reflections on the state of our health care industry, as well as universal themes on human nature."

—Lindsay Morgan

"I was intrigued with the concept of this book even before it was published. How would you handle knowing your blood was unique in that it could heal the deadliest diseases? Miss Onuorah handled the subject in a way that kept me glued to the pages and anticipating the next chapter. With unexpected plot twists and interesting characters, I was surprised, shocked and ultimately rewarded with a satisfying outcome. Well done!"

—Salli Siddle Anderson

Type N

A novel

Michelle N. Onuorah

Type N
Published by MNO Media, LLC
La Mirada, CA 90638 U.S.A.

ISBN-13: 978-0615812458
ISBN-10: 0615812457

Please note there is occasional cursing, violence, and reference to spirituality within this work of fiction. If any of the above or the mixture of the above offend you, you have been warned.

Cover Design by Beverly Arce
Formatting by Polgarus Studio

DEDICATION

I want to thank my family:
My mom, Dr. Victoria Oshodi and my dad, Mr. Sylvester Onuorah
Natalie, Daniel, and Ford – thanks for being such great siblings.
Auntie Eni – thanks for helping me with the design concept.
My grandmothers: Mrs. Florence Oshodi and Mrs. Gold Lucy Onuorah –
thanks for your support and love.
The rest of my family – you know who you are and I love you.

Friends – both personal and professional:
Chavonte Harris, Irma Costantino, Dominique Henry, Kelly Holmberg,
Dannica Anderson (your generosity still amazes me!)
Gabriella Odudu – thank you for keeping me excited about this.
Agam and Oge – and my nieces and nephew thanks to you two.
Sharon Kinard – thank you for being so encouraging and loving.
Mrs. Leanna Willis, Kay Henry, Doretha O'Quinn, Katrina Greene
Deborah Taylor, Dorothy Scharer, Tiffany Castro, Matt Barber, Salli Jo
Anderson, Octavio Martinez, Donald Gordon
Terry of Wexford, Sith Riantawan and Joy Riantawan

Kickstarter Buddies:
Thank you to everyone who donated to the fund. You know who you are
and I truly do appreciate you. Without your help, I wouldn't have had
the time, space, or resources to write this book.

My Lord and Savior, Jesus Christ

CHAPTER ONE

Nicolette:

I run. I run as hard as I can in the middle of the forest, cell phone pasted to my ear. I run so hard my chest feels like an inferno. I ignore the burn.

It's the dead of night, and I can hear shouting in the distance pierced every now and then by the dogs barking.

"Information. How can I help you?" the operator asks.

"I need the address for 206-555-6484. Hurry, please!"

Flashlights circle behind me, and I try to run even faster. Suddenly, I lose my footing and trip over an unseen root, cell phone flying out of my hand. I gasp in pain but get back up and scramble to find the phone. There is no time for pain, barely time for running. I find it just as the operator pulls the address.

"1504 Menlee Drive," she rattles off. I shut the phone and take off again.

My race leads me to a residential area. I squint at the little numbers on the street curbs until I find the house I'm looking for and bang on the door. A tall, very young, blonde hair, blue-eyed man opens it. He takes one look at me and wordlessly lets me in.

One Year, Four Months Earlier:

If I, Nicolette Talloway, could sum up my day-to-day existence in one word, it would be isolated. At school, I go through my day surrounded by people yet entirely alone. Sometimes I feel like if it weren't for the numerous records of my existence, I would literally vaporize from the consciousness of those around me. How do I begin to describe myself to you?

Let's start with the basics: I am a seventeen-year-old junior at Bellmont High School. I make good grades, go to school every day, and always sit in the corner of class. I'm the kid who was just *too something*: too weird, too skinny, too tall, too pale. Never cool enough to be noticed, but not strange enough to be picked on. Growing up, sometimes I envied the kids that got bullied.

At least they were seen.

Nothing is out of the norm today. I wake up, get on the bus, and go to school. I go through classes taking notes, watching the idiotic behavior of my clown classmates, virtually invisible. It's quite entertaining actually. Some of my classmates are straight jackasses but some of them really could have a career in comedy. I walk down the hallways, into the bathroom, into the cafeteria... alone, alone, alone. My favorite place to be is the library. During lunch, I sit in the almost-empty room of books and switch between reading my book, drawing in my sketchpad and observing the people who pass by outside.

People-watching has always been one of my favorite hobbies. By watching the habits and outlines of others, I'm better able to mimic them in my art. Not that I'm a real "artist" but I'm a hell of a doodler, always drawing stuff on scraps of paper and convincing myself that I know what I'm doing. It also helps being inconsequential to others because they never notice me watching them.

People tend to look over me, past me, or right through me. And making friends is easier said than done. Sometimes I feel like friendship is a train that everyone hopped on and for some reason I missed it and am still standing on the platform.

At home, life isn't that different. My family has gotten used to my withdrawn nature and stopped trying to draw and include me in their conversations years ago. As long as I'm not pregnant or doing drugs, my parents aren't concerned. If I were carved out of the picture, my family would be the embodiment of 1950s Americana.

My parents are an average-attractive couple in their forties; my father an accountant, my mother an interior designer. Our house was built from scratch with an open floor plan and practically reeks of upper-middle class money. It is both modern and warm with beige, bronze, and orange hues. We sit around the dark oak table in the dining room adjoining the kitchen. Conversation swirls around me like normal.

"How are classes, Nat?" Mom asks.

"So far so good," she replies. "I'm on the weekly rotation now. No more reporting about dances and crap. My team got assigned to the elections."

My older sister, Natalia, is a blonde bombshell who blows every dumb blonde stereotype out of the water. A junior at the University of Washington, she is at the top of her class and is on the fast track to a promising career in journalism.

"All right!" Dad exclaims.

"Congratulations, sis." Nate winks at her.

My younger brother, Nathaniel, is an equally attractive, amiable guy. He's just a year younger than me and my parents have strong hopes for him, their only son. I guess you could say he is the poster child for courage and strength and the only family member who ever sees me on occasion. Every now and then, I catch him watching me with half concern, half curiosity. Sometimes he'll even ask me how I'm doing. That's just him…he's…nice.

"Thanks," Natalia replies. "Call it the benefits of being an upperclassman at UW. *Finally* we get to-"

My brother starts coughing incessantly. He looks at my sister apologetically but we all know that he can't help it. He can never anticipate when it's going to come. Mom rushes to the kitchen. Dad clasps my brother by the back of the neck, as if to brace him for the coughs racking his body.

Growing up, Nate has always had a string of illnesses, combined with chronic asthma. Between my parents' constant praise and adoration of Natalia and their pride mingled with concern for Nathaniel, I know they have nothing left in the emotional bank for me. Middle-child syndrome, I guess.

"How bad this time?" Natalia asks Nate.

He holds up seven digits.

"I'll get his medicine." She takes off without another word. Mom returns with an inhaler and pops it in his mouth.

"Top shelf in the pantry," she calls out to my sister.

Nate deeply inhales and his cough begins to subside.

"Does this have anything to do with…?" Dad asks.

"I guess we'll find out next week," Mom replies.

"What if she doesn't know?"

"Tom, she's the top oncologist in the country. Of course she'll know."

"But is melanoma her specialty?"

"She'll know, Tom!"

Yeah.

His latest challenge has been his recent bout with melanoma. I look at Nate, my worries stamped all over my face. He catches my eye and winks in assurance as if to say, *"I'll be fine."*

Two Weeks Later

"Hello?"

"Nikki, it's Mom. We need you to get to the Wakefield ER as soon as possible."

I glance at the clock which reads 8:35. My whole family is usually home by six at the latest.

"Why? What happened? Are you okay?"

"It's not me," Mom explains. "It's Nate. He's been in a car accident, and he needs blood. We've all been tested but none of us are O negative. Rebecca Jensen is but she's too anemic to donate. We need you to get tested right away."

My mother hangs up before I can get another word in.

The deluge of shock, worry, and anger hits me like a wave against the shore. Of all the people to get in an accident, did it really have to be my brother? Mom mentioned the Jensens. How could she and Dad have contacted them before calling me? I'm his sister. I'm seventeen. I'm not in college or grad school or some other state, married with two kids. I'm still a member of the nuclear family unit. Why didn't my family contact me earlier? How is it that I am just getting this news now?

As I drive to the hospital, the questions don't cease and as the questions mount, my anger rises. I can't help but stack my family's offenses the way a miser stacks his coins. I'm furious with them, and I'm beginning to wonder if my family would show nearly the same amount of concern if it were me in that hospital bed. I also wonder how many people already know. Who else have they called?

When I arrive at the hospital, my premonition is validated. Teachers, students, neighbors, and distant relatives crowd the hospital waiting room. The whole town knew of my brother's accident before I did. I approach the mob, fully aware that I am the last person anyone thought to call in this emergency.

I gaze around the room and catch my older sister's eye.

"Nikki!" Natalia exclaims. My parents' heads snap in my direction, and they rush over to me.

"Thank God you're finally here. What took you so long?" Mom says. She kisses my cheek absentmindedly and takes my bag out of my hand.

I squelch my urge to ask her, *"Are you kidding me? What took you so long?"*

I turn to my father. "Dad, how is he?"

He kisses my forehead but doesn't answer my question.

"You're here now, that's all that matters." Dad pulls off my coat and flings it on a chair. They usher me to the nearby nurse and I suddenly realize that they just tag-teamed me! The nurse's station is a mess. Telephones keep ringing, women and men in scrubs rush all around us. My dad singles out one of them.

"Nurse," Dad says. "This is our other daughter. Please test her too."

He waits a moment.

"Now," he clarifies.

The nurse looks like someone wrung her through an old fashioned washing machine. My parents aren't difficult people but they can be demanding when they are stressed.

"Mr. Talloway, I will test your daughter as soon as possible-"

"Why can't you do it now?"

"Mr. Talloway, there are other patients in this hospital-"

"Are there other patients with melanoma who have just been in a serious wreck? Test her blood now, please!"

The nurse opens her mouth to respond, but my father gives her such a searing look of warning that she begins to look around for help.

"Don't worry, Jan. Jason will test her."

An average-looking, middle-aged man with brown hair gestures to a tall blonde guy in a white lab coat. The blonde guy extends his hand to me.

"Dr. Jason Monroe. I'm assisting Dr. McGrath," he gestures to the older gentleman, "in treating your brother."

Okay, I know I'm in the ER and this is a total emergency but I can't help but notice how good-looking this guy is. His eyes are a deep blue. Not sky blue or baby blue, but ice glazier water blue. He has a straight nose, sharp jaw line, and a full head of silky blonde hair. Even worse, as I lean in to take his hand, I'm met with a cool, refreshing scent that must be his cologne. His presence is so disarming, I have to look away. *Please don't let him see how nervous I am.* This is too much. My brother's in the hospital, my family didn't have the decency to call me until just now – and now I have to deal with a ridiculously attractive man.

"Please follow me."

"Thank you, Doctor." Dad says appreciatively.

This man looks *way* too young to be a doctor. If I could guess, I would say he's only a couple years older than me, but I silently follow him to a nearby lab room. They already have my file on hand and my thoughts switch back to my parents and the situation at hand. My anger begins to surge through me to the point where I can barely hold my arm still for the needle. As Dr. Sex-on-a-Stick draws my blood, I can only think of how my family has slighted me. Is it irrational to be upset? When an emergency takes place, aren't you supposed to contact loved ones? Or am I not a loved one even in my own family?

CHAPTER TWO

Jason:

Nicolette Talloway. She's upset. I mean, why wouldn't she be? Her brother is in the hospital, having suffered a serious accident. The kid is lucky to be alive. She seems more angry than distraught though. I'm running the test for her blood but all I can think about is how she had remained completely silent when I drew it, taking deep breaths to stay composed. The test will take almost an hour to complete so I decide to do some rounds in the meantime.

I take the long route and stop at the nurse's station near the waiting room to pick up my charts. I don't know why – okay that's bull, I do know why. I want to see her. I try my best to be inconspicuous as I observe her. She sits completely removed from her family. There is a huge crowd surrounding her, yet no one seems to notice her. Her arms are crossed and her head is down like it was in the phlebotomy room.

She has long, jet black hair that curls at the edges. Her skin is really pale – but it suits her. Long dark lashes shield her eyes from the outside world, and I wish I could have gotten her attention, if only to see her eyes for a second. *So this is what Snow White looks like.* Snow White could use a cheeseburger.

Or five.

When I first saw her in her black attire, I thought she was trying to make a statement and stand out from her American pie family, but on second thought, I don't think so. Most Goth chicks would go for combat boots to finish off their look; instead she's wearing plain black running shoes. I can't see her eyes, but her straight nose, full lips, and high cheek bones indicate that she's just as beautiful as her sister if not more. Frankly, she's stunning, and she's not even trying. I feel like a pedophile watching her but I remind myself that I'm twenty and only three years ago, it was totally legal for me to dig a chick her age.

But that was three years ago.

Why is she sitting by herself? Why is no one in the room even acknowledging her? Her mother, father, and sister are all huddled together, giving each other hugs and words of encouragement. Did she get in a fight with them? Shouldn't an emergency like this squash any petty family dispute? And if she did get in a fight with them, what of the others in the room? She can't have alienated herself from the *entire town*. Watching her, I can't help but feel a deep sense of empathy. I feel a burning in my chest that is much akin to anger. What the hell is wrong with these people?

"Jason!"

I jump when I feel a meaty hand clap me hard on my back. I *hate* it when people do that. Hurts my back and scares the crap out of me at the same time. I turn to my supervisor and mentor, Dr. Greg McGrath. His brown eyes are crinkled in amusement and I can already feel the heat rising to my face. He caught me.

"No time to be in la-la-land, son. Even when there is a pretty girl."

He winks at me good-naturedly. I glance over his shoulder at Nicolette and to my surprise, and relief, her mother gets up, walks over to her daughter and crouches before her. They start talking. I can almost see the gratitude on the girl's face, and I'm glad.

I give Greg a curt nod. Staring stops now.

I force myself to take my chart and keep walking. I try, and fail, to stifle a yawn. I chalk it up to fatigue. I'm working a double shift. I'm exhausted and irritated; therefore my head isn't screwed on right. I stop at a water fountain and splash my face to wake up but my mind won't leave the waiting room. *How is this any of my business?* When an hour has passed, I stride over to the lab and look over the results. What the-?

This can't be right.

I turn to a nearby nurse.

"Carla, please page Dr. McGrath for me."

I turn back to the results. This can't be right.

Nicolette:

I wish I brought a book with me. Or my sketchpad. This is like school all over again except more stressful. Everyone won't stop talking and talking and talking to each other. I suppose mindless chatter eases some people's nerves but it just puts mine on edge. I think about my brother. Lying in a bed somewhere in this building but we have no access to him. All we know is that he's alive.

For now.

They say his blood is O negative, that he can only receive the same blood type. I find it ironic that he can give his blood to any human being but is the most exclusive in terms of accepting blood. I've picked up a lot from overhearing several conversations at once. Apparently my brother was heading to the mall with some friends and got t-boned by a red-light runner. He took most of the impact and his friends had minor injuries. The idiot who hit him is sitting in a jail cell and good riddance.

I've also learned that the latest stock of O negative ran out earlier this morning. Another shipment is on the way. I wish I could see him. I wish he didn't climb into that car or cross that intersection at the very second he did. I wish it were me in the driver's seat. To my surprise, I see a pair of feet walking in my direction. My mother crouches before me and rubs my lap absentmindedly. I was really beginning to think I was invisible.

She wonders aloud, "What's taking them so long? They should have the results by now. I can't stand this waiting."

So that's what she's approached me for? To air out her frustrations?

"Speaking of waiting," I venture. "Why did it take you and Dad so long to contact me about Nate?"

My mom looks up at me in surprise. I don't mean to sound so accusatory. In fact, I've been restraining myself from broaching the topic for the past hour. I couldn't look at, much less, talk to my family without feeling the anger gnaw at my gut and I know my question has a bit of a bite in its delivery. My mom is still pondering my question, her frown pinching even harder. She stops frowning after a while and looks me in the eye with all sincerity.

"Nicolette, I am so sorry. I won't even begin to add insult to injury by trying to explain what we were thinking. We weren't. We just..." she trails off, trying to find the right words.

"You just forgot about me."

It's not a question.

I guess my mother can see the hurt on my face even though I'm doing my best to hide it. She grabs my hands.

"Nikki-"

"Mrs. Talloway? Mr. Talloway?" Dr. McGrath and his intern approach us with strange looks on their faces. *Great timing, Doc.* My mother's attention immediately shifts to him and the whole room hushes in rapt attention.

"Mr. and Mrs. Talloway," he begins. "We are sorry for the wait. After testing your daughter's blood we discovered some unusual results."

"Nothing to worry about," he says at their worried expressions. "We were just wondering if it would be possible to get another sample of her blood and cross-check the results."

My parents immediately acquiesce to the request without even glancing in my direction. I'm about to look back down when I notice the doctor standing slightly behind Dr. McGrath. A slight look of annoyance crosses his face at my parents' automatic permission. Why would he be annoyed? Aren't they giving him what he and his supervisor wants? It's as if he feels indignant on my behalf. His eyes snap to mine and I quickly look down, too nervous to look back up as I stand to follow them into the lab room. My brother is running out of time. The sooner they discover a match, the better.

Jason:

Hazel. Her eyes are hazel. She looked at me. It was only for a brief second but I can still feel the rush of excitement at catching her gaze. The three of us: Greg, Nicolette, and I walk down the hall to the phlebotomy room. This time Greg draws the blood himself. I'm not offended. I need to know if I made a mistake the first time or if her blood really is as strange as I'm thinking. Greg tries to make small talk with her but quickly gives up after a string of softly-spoken one word answers. She keeps her eyes focused on her arm the entire time and refuses to make eye contact with either of us when it's over. She finds her own way back to the waiting room.

"Strange girl," he mutters. I bristle at the comment.

"Her brother's in critical condition. How can she be normal right now?" I respond in a sharp tone. He puts his hands up in mock defense and takes the blood to the lab. I decide to make my rounds without stopping by the waiting room this time. By the time I round the corner from my last check in, Greg is hot on my heels. He practically yanks me into the lab and lays out the results.

"Come again?" Mr. Talloway responds in disbelief. His wife puts her hand on his shoulder with the same look of incredulity.

"I said your daughter doesn't have a blood type. Or at least not a blood type known to medical record," Greg explains. "She's not A, B, AB, or O and her Rh results are inconclusive."

"So…you don't even know if her blood is positive or negative?" Natalia asked.

"Correct," I respond. "We tested Miss Talloway's blood on several different machines and even forwarded her blood at our own expense to a nearby hematologist. Your daughter has a blood type. Just not one previously recorded."

I watch her family take it in. Nicolette does not look pleased. She's not panicked or shocked like I would expect her to be but looks more annoyed at her medical anomaly. She's so different. Her parents and sister are flailing about like nervous rats in a maze but she remains steady. Calm. Her brows are stitched together in a thoughtful frown and to everyone's surprise she speaks.

"What now?" she asks softly. "Nate is still in critical condition and he needs blood. What now?"

She looks at us imploringly. Her parents turn to us.

"Your daughter's right," Greg says. "Your son is running out of time. I don't know anything about your daughter's blood except that it comes from a healthy donor and a blood relative of your son. We can't use any of your or your eldest daughter's blood. You have three options. You can have your neighbor's highly anemic daughter donate her blood – which could kill him because of its iron levels; you could risk waiting until an O negative shipment comes through. Or you can take a risk and see if your daughter's blood may help her brother."

Mrs. Talloway looks like she's on the verge of an emotional breakdown. She tucks her head into her husband's shoulders and softly cries. Mr. Talloway holds his wife and looks at his youngest daughter.

He then asks Greg, "What are the chances of Jenny Jensens' blood killing our son?"

My supervisor's eyes widen in surprise.

"If she were mildly anemic or even moderately anemic, I would say around forty-five percent," he answers. "But this girl is on the verge of acute anemia and has around a seventy percent chance of adding toxicity to your son's blood –"

"Let alone risking her own health in donating," I add.

"No amount of iron tablets can turn her iron levels around in time. You daughter's blood on the other hand has a-"

"Fifty-fify shot," Mr. Talloway interrupts. "Use her blood," he says decisively. His wife jerks her head up from his shoulder and stares at him.

"Are you sure?" she asks.

"Nate has a better chance with Nikki's blood than Jenny's. Fifty is better than thirty."

Wow. What a mechanical, pragmatic way to look at things. For a second, it looks like his wife is about to slap him but she takes a deep breath, lowers her eyes, and nods her head in agreement. Once again, I notice that neither of them thinks to ask Nicolette about the decision. She stands and looks me in the eye for the second time.

"Let's do it."

CHAPTER THREE

Nicolette:

It worked. Or at least I think it did. One pint, two hours and a bunch of gauze later – my brother is still alive. The first rays of dawn hit his face which barely has any scratches. Looking at him, no one would have guessed he had just survived a near-fatal wreck. The worry lines on my parents' faces have diminished and my sister has felt confident enough of the situation to finally grab us all some food from the cafeteria.

My parents and I are in his room with him and there is a constant flurry of scrubs and white coats coming in and out. As long as he is still alive, I'm satisfied. The sun is beginning to rise and though my hips and bottom ache from sitting in this cold metal chair all night, I feel the lightness in my spirit matches the light pouring into the room.

It feels like the calm after the storm or the light at the end of the tunnel or all those other clichéd analogies used to describe things finally getting better. I actually want things to go back to normal even if it means returning to the dull reality of my desolation. I can bear my emotional torment but not the physical ones of my family. My parents finally nod off and I decide to stretch my legs and walk around. I quietly leave the room and go exploring. This hospital is like one giant maze. I'm pretty good at maintaining my orientation and make visits everywhere from the maternity ward to the psychiatric wing. I should have known there would be ample content for people-watching in a hospital. I'm about to make my way back to Nate's room when I hear a rush of voices in a nearby lounge. I recognize a couple of them.

"His level and speed of recovery is unprecedented. His vitals started stabilizing within thirty minutes of the transfusion and there was no trace of internal bleeding after forty-five minutes. McGrath, what did you give that kid?"

"I told you," Dr. McGrath responds. *"It was his other sister's blood. We still don't know what type it is or how to categorize it. I'm just glad he's recovering. Can you imagine if his reaction had been the opposite?"*

"Class action malpractice suit."

"I thought you got the parents to sign a liability waiver."

"Please, do you know how many loopholes a malpractice attorney can use to maneuver around that?"

"Hey!"

I whip around, surprised. My eyes snap up to a pair of cobalt blue peekers. It's him. Nate's other doctor. I feel flustered all over again. Not only is this guy incredibly good-looking, he just caught me eavesdropping into a conversation that was totally not my business. I look down on impulse and begin to walk away.

"Sorry," I mutter, hoping to escape. *Leave me alone, leave me alone, leave me alone...* I feel his strong hand grasp my arm.

"Whoa, hold on," he says in a voice light with laughter. I turn. He lets go of my arm. "You're not in trouble or anything. I listen in all the time."

"But you're their colleague." I study the dated patterns on the tile floor.

"I know. That makes it even worse."

I look up at him. He's grinning a careless smile like something is tickling him. I can't imagine what it is. Is he enjoying my discomfort?

"Doctor –"

"Please," he holds his hand up. "Call me Jason."

I frown at him. Most doctors don't go by a first-name basis.

"Jason, how old are you?"

He grins again.

"Why?"

"You look-"

"Too young?" he guesses.

I nod. He smiles again and walks around me.

"See you around, Nicolette."

As I make my way back to the room, I hear voices much more familiar than Dr. McGrath's.

"Nate!" I exclaim and rush into the room. My brother is sitting up in his bed, his eyes alert, with a welcoming smile on his face. I scurry over to the bed and gently give him a hug. I'm surprised at how strong his embrace is in return. I take a second look at him. He doesn't just look good. He looks amazing. It's like seeing a before and after picture spaced out by only a few minutes.

He and my parents continue their conversation but I can't even jump in – not that I normally would – because I'm too busy observing him. Not only are his eyes alert, the color has returned to his face and his bruises seem to have faded into a much lighter shade of purple. I can't seem to put my finger on the biggest change I notice until it hits me.

"You're not wheezing," I interrupt the conversation. My parents and brother look confused at first but the realization soon dawns on them as they listen harder for my brother's patented wheeze. Nathaniel himself looks amazed.

"You're right, sis." He closes his eyes and takes a deep breath. "So this is what it feels like to breathe without any effort." My mother's eyes well with tears as she rises to give him another hug. My dad, though happy, looks a little perplexed and I know what he's thinking. How is it that my brother is healing so well, so rapidly?

"Hello, Nathaniel," Dr. McGrath greets us warmly. "It's good to see you recovering so well."

And so quickly, I might add. After a series of tests, the doctor gives my brother the green light.

He's free to go home.

"Just make sure you take him to his oncologist as soon as possible."

"He's actually scheduled to see her in a couple of weeks. Is that soon enough?" my father asks.

"I would try to get him in sooner after what he's gone through but," Dr. McGrath pauses, "something tells me your son will be okay either way."

He leaves the room without further instruction.

When my parents aren't gushing over me for donating or Dr. McGrath for administering care, they're busy fawning over Jason.

"Thank you so much for everything," Mom says softly.

"You're very welcome, Mrs. Talloway," Jason replies.

"Is there some way we can reach you if we have any other questions?" Dad asks.

"Yes, of course. Here's my card. My office and personal number are on there."

I think it will stop here. I've given my blood, and Nate will get better so he can continue with life as normal, recover from the accident and focus on fighting his cancer.

But I can't shake this feeling that nothing is going back to normal.

Jason:

"It's her blood," Norris insists. "There is no medicine, surgery, or apothecary miracle that can otherwise explain the boy's healing." I try to speak but Dr. Montgomery Norris, the state's top hematologist, continues.

"I would concede *if* his injuries alone were staunched and his medical condition returned to that previous of the accident. But he's not just healing. He's *thriving*! Maladies that he suffered *prior to the accident* are healing! His chronic asthma has vanished, his ribs are healed, and his left leg no longer needs a cast! Even his damn bruises are fading fast!"

"Montgom –"

"No – you give me an explanation. Any explanation. Hell, I might even start believing in that witchcraft, voodoo shit if it in some way explains this kid's one-eighty."

He pauses in all sincerity, waiting for Greg's reply. Just as he opens his mouth to respond, Norris continues with, "How much do you want to bet his cancer is gone?"

"What?"

We both look at him in shock.

"Why not? All of his other maladies have disappeared. Has he seen his oncologist?"

"Not yet," I reply. Greg looks captive in thought.

"Okay," he murmurs. "You're right. It is her blood. But you're going to have to do a hell of a lot more research to prove that it is her blood and not some other factor. The medical community will turn you out on your ear if you don't have some solid proof stacked up."

"Wait a minute," I speak up. "Medical community? Just how many people are going to know about Nicolette – I mean Miss Talloway's – blood?"

I can't put my finger on it but something just doesn't sit right with me about Norris's enthusiasm regarding her blood. I'm thrilled that her brother is getting better and that her blood turned out to be the best choice. But every milestone in his recovery further distinguishes the capabilities of her blood. What will this mean for her moving forward?

"What are we going to do now?" Greg ignores my question. "This is out of our jurisdiction. The kid is completely fine now and there's no reason to keep him here any longer."

"You're releasing him today?" Norris asks, alarmed.

"We have to."

There is a pregnant pause in the room.

"Let me talk to her then. The girl and her parents," Norris suggests.

Nicolette:

We're not going home...not yet. A new doc has entered the picture...something Norris. He's a few inches shorter than McGrath and over a head beneath Jason in stature. A balding, eager beaver in his late forties, this man has way too much energy for his age.

"Mr. and Mrs. Talloway, I recognize that this is the last place you want to be but please hear me out." the doctor pleads with an almost desperate smile.

"I have practiced medicine – specialized in hematology – for more than twenty years. I have never seen any blood sample like that of your daughter's."

He looks over at me with an expression I can't quite describe. Like he wants to consume me or something. I remind myself that he wants what's in my veins, not necessarily me but that doesn't comfort me at all.

17

Dr. McGrath speaks up, "This is somewhat unorthodox but Dr. Norris was wondering if we could contact your oncologist and have him—"

"Her," Natalia corrects.

"—her, come in and run some tests on Nathaniel. He would also like to continue examining your daughter's blood sample for further research," he finishes.

I look over his shoulder at Jason, who stands with a blank, professional expression. He catches me staring and his lips curve the slightest bit.

My dad looks at my mom with querying eyes. Mom shrugs her shoulders. I'm not surprised when they answer with:

"We'll be happy to help in any way we can. The oncologist coming over would save us the trip and we would like to find out how Nate is doing in that department sooner than later. As long as this doesn't disrupt Nikki and Nate's school work, you have our permission."

"Thank you, Mr. and Mrs. Talloway," Dr. Norris gushes. He's grinning a wide face-splitting smile, with enough excitement to cover both Jason and Dr. McGrath beside him.

They're just tests. Just blood samples. Besides me feeling the pain of more needles, there shouldn't be any major sacrifices on my part. Yet for some reason, I can't shake this feeling of foreboding.

Something tells me Dr. Norris did a little arm wrestling to get the oncologist in this morning. Dr. White, an attractive brunette in her mid-fifties, has "hassled" written all over her face. Though polite, she's very short with Nate and my parents, initially asking questions in a brief, succinct voice, almost as if she doesn't want to waste an unnecessary breath on any unnecessary syllables. To be fair, she probably has numerous patients in her own clinic, waiting to be seen. The more she observes my brother, however, the more she slows down.

I can see it in her face.

I had the same expression only hours ago. Her eyes widen in amazement as she tests his strength and dexterity. She takes care to personally draw his blood. We have yet to hear from her.

My sister stretches in visible irritation.

"What's taking her so long?"

I shrug. "She's probably running several tests at once."

"No, Nat's right," Mom says. "Even when we're at her clinic, the tests take a fraction of the amount of time she's spent. I hope there's nothing wrong," she says in a worried tone.

"Mom, I feel great," Nate tells her in assurance. "I've never felt this good in my life. Whatever the result, I'll take it over feeling the way I felt two days ago."

The door swings open.

Dr. White, Dr. Norris, Dr. McGrath, and Jason all stride in to Nate's little hospital room. I have never seen so many white lab coats congregated at one time. Dr. Norris has a wild look of happiness in his eyes. He keeps looking at me and it's really starting to get on my nerves. I ignore him. Dr. McGrath has a more controlled expression but I can still see something is up. Jason can certainly keep a poker face. It's Dr. White's expression that has us all waiting with bated breath.

Her eyes circle wildly in her head.

"I don't know how this happened," she says. "I've run the tests over and over and over again."

"We *know*," Natalia quips sarcastically.

"Natalia!" Mom admonishes.

"What's the news, doctor?" Dad asks, frowning in concern.

"There is no trace of his cancer."

"What?" My sister straightens in her seat. My parents' jaws hang ajar. Nate leans closer to the doctor and says:

"Can you say that again, please?"

"There is no trace of your cancer," Dr. White repeats. She looks at all of us. "I reviewed the results of his samples numerous times and then couriered the sample to a most trusted colleague. Never in my thirty years as an oncologist have I seen this type of turn-around. I've reviewed his charts. Nathaniel's blood count is better than it was prior to his diagnosis."

My dad sits back in his chair at a loss for words. Natalia seems completely out of it and Mom looks like she's about to cry.

"Nathaniel, how do you feel?" Dr. McGrath asks.

"Great now!" he replies. The doctors chuckle in amusement.

"Thank you for your patience and your willingness to stay a few more hours. I've given the nurses notice. You are free to go home."

"And I will be in touch with you shortly," Dr. Norris interjects, eyes darting from my parents to me. The last thing I want to do is see this creep again. But something tells me it's no longer an option.

CHAPTER FOUR

Several Months Later

Nicolette:

His cancer is gone.

There's no such thing as normal. I think it's well established that I am a cynical, easily-irritated pessimist but I'm trying to look on the bright side here. It feels like we took my brother home a lifetime ago – so much has changed. He's healthy. For once his physical condition matches his bigger than life personality. He's into sports now and goes biking with my dad. All the things he couldn't do before, he's taking them on as if he's making up for lost time.

His cancer is gone.

It's great and I'm happy for him. But while his life gets to go back to normal, my life has gotten very strange very fast. I've never met so many different oncologists and hematologists and whatever-ists in my life – all of them with this greedy look of excitement in their eyes, silently pleading with me to give them something I don't even know I have.

I've become well-acquainted with needles.

As I walk into the research center, I try to prepare myself for what I know is ahead. I take the elevator trip, walk down the hall, past the receptionist and into my usual room. I sit on the squeaky leather chair and wait for the vampire of the hour.

For the past year, specialists have routinely taken samples of my blood to test on patients with some illness. During the first trial, they told me the procedure in detail: ten patients had the same disease; five got my blood, the other five thought they got my blood but got some placebo version. The five who got my blood improved and the other five didn't, therefore something about my blood is medicinal. We have gone through fourteen trials so far with different patients and different diseases. Time and time again, my blood has seemed to cure the patients of whatever ailment they have.

This explains so much. Growing up, I took it for granted that I didn't catch colds. I've never had the flu. I don't even know what chicken pox would feel like. When people cough around me, I don't get nervous or ask them to cover their mouths. I don't worry because I've never caught anything from anyone before. When flues or colds would take out my entire family, I would rise and shine and head to school, the only one unscathed. Now it all makes sense.

Being the main source of a research team's testing material is exhausting. I used to have fantasies of what it would be like to be noticed and recognized by others. Now that it's a reality, I'd rather go back to my life pre-Nate's accident. If only I knew what I had when I had it. Privacy, for one thing. The ability to disappear for another. And at least back then, I had more time with my family. I miss having them talk over my head about everything I couldn't care less about. Now I have to listen to complete strangers talk over my head about shit I *really* couldn't care less about.

No one in this lab really talks to me. If they do, it's only to say, "Hold still." "Make a fist." "Okay, release the fist." "Here's some water." "Not feeling light-headed, are you?"

I spin in circles as the leather chair squeaks. Someone enters the room as my back faces the door. *Three...two...one...*

"You know you might give yourself a headache if you do that too long," a wry, amused voice says.

I whip around and face the door.

"Jason!"

He smiles and pulls up a chair of his own.

Thank God for Jason. He's one of the leaders on the research team with Dr. Norris. From what I understand, most of his work involves the analysis of my blood and working with the patients who receive it. But he still comes around to check on me and I'm grateful to see a friendly face.

"How are you?" he asks. And it doesn't feel like a formality. He actually wants to know how I'm doing.

"I'm okay," I quickly answer. He cocks his head and looks at me for a few moments.

"In all the time I've known you, you've never not been 'okay.'"

"What am I supposed to say? 'My life is so miserable, I contemplated suicide again?'" I retort.

His eyebrows shoot up in surprise.

"I hope you would. If that's what you really were going through." He stops and looks at me seriously for a moment. "Are you going through that, Nic?"

He calls me Nic. No one in my family calls me that. But I like that he does. I have a hard time reading him. He's joking and kind one minute, then serious and deep the next. I've never had a boyfriend but if there really is something called a woman's intuition and I have it, I would say he's interested in me. But just when my suspicions are about to be confirmed, he flips the switch and goes back into professional, doctor-mode.

I shut him out.

"I'm fine, Jason. Are you drawing the blood or is someone else today?"

He leans back and looks me over like he knows something is up. I keep silent and so does he. We can do this all day long.

He gets up, pats the patient bed. I sit on it, roll up my left sleeve and stick out my pocked and bruised left arm. The drill is so natural, it barely hurts anymore. He draws the blood and releases the tourniquet on my arm. Stores the sample, places the needle in a sharps container and throws the gloves in the biohazard bin. He heads over to the door but turns before opening it, concern still written on his face.

"You have my number, right?"

I nod.

"Don't be afraid to use it."

With that, he leaves the room.

206-555-6484

Ten digits I can't seem to forget.

Present

Jason:

"One year," I repeat to the reporter. "We studied Nicolette Talloway's blood for one year."

The conference room should have been large enough for the amount of press we invited but I can already sympathize with the claustrophobic in this stagnant mass of bodies. I can feel the heat from the bulbs of the light fixtures. Boom operators invade my space with their fuzzy-topped friends. I have never seen so many reporters in one room.

They are all here to hear what my colleagues and I have discovered.

"It's her blood," Norris insists. I try to speak but Norris continues.

"Hours before Nathaniel Talloway checked out of the hospital, his oncologist ran tests only to discover that his stage three melanoma was completely gone. His sudden recovery combined with Miss Talloway's blood typing anomaly prompted Dr. McGrath and Dr. Monroe to team up with me and other researchers to study Miss Talloway's blood."

"The results were consistent," I jump in. "Even as the patient makeup changed: from cancer to HIV/AIDS to Parkinson's – during the clinical trials every single patient given Miss Talloway's blood was cured."

The cameras click more rapidly. Some of the reporters look dumfounded, others more skeptical. One from the latter, an auburn-haired, middle aged woman, raises her hand.

"How is it that you are just discovering Miss Talloway's blood anomaly now?" she asks with a critical frown. "Aren't all babies tested for their blood type at birth?"

"Not necessarily," I respond. "Nicolette's mother opted for a natural home birth. Her daughter was deemed healthy and there was not a necessity to type her blood at a nearby hospital."

She nods, seemingly satisfied. A tall, young man in his twenties raises his hand.

"You said that you first discovered her blood during a transfusion. How much of her blood is needed to cure a disease?"

Greg answers, "During the clinical, we progressively reduced the dosage of her blood in our trial patients to learn how much was required at the bare minimum. We discovered that we only need 10cc or 10mL of her blood in order to take effect, the amount that would fill most syringes."

"How is this even medically possible?" a short, balding reporter jumps in. "Aren't there certain proteins that determine a person's blood type?"

"We discovered that Miss Talloway's blood contains an extra protein," Norris answers. "There are five commonly known plasma proteins: albumins, immunoglobulins, fibrinogens, alpha 1-antitrypsin, and regulatory proteins," he explains. "Her blood contains a protein that does not fit into any known category. It functions entirely on its own. When confronted with an antigen of any sort, it immediately clones itself, disburses, and consumes every single antigen present."

"What does any of that have to do with typing?" the reporter interjects.

"She has a blood type," Norris asserts. "Just not one previously recorded. Her blood functions like an O negative in that it is a universal donor. However, it is also a universal recipient."

"That's not possible," the reporter scoffs.

I restrain the urge to ask where he got his MD and patiently explain:

"With her protein, it is. This particular protein will neutralize and synthesize any blood she receives and make it amenable for her body's needs."

"So when people receive her blood, does their type change to hers?"

"No," Greg responds. "It replicates itself just enough to destroy the antigens already existing in the blood. After the disease or illness is completely removed, the trace of the donor blood disappears as the host blood replicates."

A different reporter, a young blonde woman, raises her hand, hope written on her face.

"The patients who receive her blood," she says. "Are they cured for life? Immune from disease?"

The reporters begin to murmur amongst themselves at the prospect of such a cure. I answer this one.

"We are still studying the long term effects of the blood. Cellular diseases such as cancer have not re-emerged, nor have any of the diseases cured." I add, "One hundred percent of the patients who received the blood have reported high levels of energy, improved sleep, and strengthened immune systems. Miss Talloway's brother has yet to receive a cold, cough or flu since his transfusion."

"Is it possible to replicate this protein?"

There's a pregnant pause in the air. I look down at my notes and back up to the sea of cameras and mics. This is what I've been trying to avoid, been working so hard to find a solution to. I know with this one word, Nicolette's life will never be the same again. Here goes...

"No," I admit. "It is not possible to replicate this protein or make any sort of synthetic version of it at this time."

"So you would need this girl... this... Nicolette Talloway... to provide her blood, the cure, on a regular basis?"

"Correct."

When the press conference breaks, I get up to make my escape. Reporters and their mics crowd in on my personal space. Some of these people should really use deodorant before coming to a conference like this. I push my way through the crowd, ignoring the questions screamed in my ear. It's all white noise anyway. The sea of faces give way to a break in the room as the reporters turn back to a more-than-willing Norris to get their questions satisfied. The only face I can think of is hers.

What the hell did I just do to this girl and her family?

Nicolette:

"We never should have consented to that press conference," Mom says to Dad, hand covering the cell phone pasted to her ear.

"Something tells me they would have released the news regardless of our consent," Dad replies. "At least we knew ahead of time. Can you imagine if we didn't?"

It's a madhouse here.

A phone-ringing, door-knocking, press-surrounding madhouse. It's been two hours since the press conference aired and there has been no peace. They warned us. They told us what to expect. Even got the local police to keep watch over the perimeter of the house but that still hasn't been enough. All of us are on the main floor of the house. Nate and Natalia switch between various news channels: all of them repeating the information in the press conference, discussing my blood, and discussing me.

CNN, Fox, ABC, MSNBC – all of them are covering the same story: me and my blood.

"For those of you just joining us on CNN," the female reporter opens. "Researchers at the Wakefield General Hospital Center for Hematology have just announced that the cure for cancer has been discovered."

There's footage of Jason talking to the press, Dr. Norris gloating over the discovery, and Dr. McGrath discussing the implications of the research.

"After a much-guarded, year-long research, scientists have concluded that an 18-year-old by the name of Nicolette Talloway carries the cure to cancer, HIV/AIDS, and other previously incurable diseases *in her blood*," she adds emphatically.

"People world-wide are celebrating the discovery," the reporter continues. "According to one source, the White House is flooded with congratulations from members of the UN."

Other footage shows people from France to Australia to Kenya to Iran dancing in the street and rejoicing in the news. There's even footage of what looks like a candlelight vigil in the Vatican City; Muslims bowing in mosques.

"Pope Francis has issued a statement encouraging Catholics and other followers of the Christian faith to 'Thank and offer the most profound gratitude to the Heavenly Father for blessing his people with the best gift given since Christ himself.'"

"Wow," Nate murmurs.

"Holy shit," Natalia gasps. "The *pope* had something to say on this? You're in the big leagues now."

I don't respond. I'm speechless.

Nate looks over at me and whispers something to Natalia. To my relief, she gets up, goes over to the TV, pops in a DVD and they watch a movie instead of various newsreels. They appear calm and try to joke around but I can tell they're more tense than normal. I don't look at them but I can feel their eyes continuously drifting to my corner. Occasionally, their eyes drift over to the dining room where our parents pace back and forth, cell phones in hand.

"What is my recourse, Jack?" Dad asks impatiently. "No, I haven't signed anything that hasn't been read by you."

"'A bidding war?'" Mom repeats. "We are not putting my daughter's *blood* up for auction. How can you even suggest that?"

"We're scheduled to meet with some rep from the FDA this evening," my dad continues. "Of course I won't sign anything. No, I don't need you there. It's only a preliminary —"

Someone knocks on the door in a loud, but specific, pattern. We all recognize the knock. The police went over it with us a thousand times. We all look at each other in unspoken apprehension.

"Jack, let me call you back." Dad hangs up. He walks over to the tall oak door, peeks through the peephole before unlocking it. A police officer in full uniform steps in.

"Thank you, Mr. Talloway." He looks around the room. "How are you all holding up?"

We nod as if to say we're okay.

"Good." His eyes linger on me a slight second longer than the rest.

"Good," he repeats. "I just wanted to inform you that the President has advised an upgrade in security for you and your family. By Governor Inslee's orders, the National Guard will be here in approximately twenty minutes to assume authority over your protection."

"The National Guard?" Mom repeats in a concerned tone. "Did the Governor declare a state of emergency?"

"No, Mrs. Talloway. However, Governor Inslee has expressed concern over the welfare and safety of your family, particularly your daughter. I'm sure this is just a precautionary measure."

Natalia lets out a low whistle and looks over at me, one eyebrow raised.

"Your life will never be the same again," she remarks.

"Don't say that!" Mom admonishes her. My sister raises her hands in defense.

"What? It's true. When you have a gift like this, your life can never be your own."

Is she right? Am I duty-bound to give up my entire life because I have something that can help others? Are my life plans and goals automatically vetoed as a result?

"Sounds more like a curse to me," my brother murmurs.

I run my hand through my hair. Why is it my curse to bear?

We've given up answering the home phone. Each time the answering machine picks up, the same plea can be heard via speaker – always a different person.

"Mr. and Mrs. Talloway," the latest voice says. "My name is Patricia Lee. My daughter Tricia attended the same high school as Nicolette. I'm sure they were friends."

Ha! Quite the opposite. I can't stand Tricia Lee.

Her mom continues, "We are so thrilled about the discovery of the cure."

That's what everyone's calling it now. My blood. The Cure.

"I know we haven't had much of a chance to connect recently," she continues.

How about ever?

"But my brother, Frank Nelson, has been battling pancreatic cancer for almost a year now and your daughter's bloo- uh...cure...is the answer to our prayers. Please give me a ring as soon as you can. 559-6284. Thanks!"

Unbelievable. Still, regardless of how I feel about Mrs. Lee or her wretched offspring, I do feel for the guy. Nobody wants cancer. Nobody wants to battle it. And the few who come out on top often have to deal with the financial and emotional mess it creates – not to mention the constant fear of it returning.

Immediately after her message drops another picks up.

"Mr. and Mrs. Talloway, this is Virginia Wane from KJLH 9," a crisp voice states. "I'm calling to see if we can arrange an interview with you and your daughter. In the meantime, we would love to get some of your initial comments in light of today's press conference. 558-2349. Thanks."

Fifteen minutes after that call and our voicemail is full.

The FDA representative looks totally at ease in my family's formal dining room. He smiles a confident grin and lays his contracts before him. He's done nothing wrong. He's been perfectly courteous and friendly, but I can't help myself.

I don't like him.

"Well, here we are," he clasps his hands. "First of all, I want to thank you for helping us wipe disease off the face of the earth. This past year has been an amazing discovery of what the blood can do." He pulls out a packet from one of the manila folders before him. I can feel the eyes of my siblings on the back of my head. Mom insisted that they stay in the living room so all they can do is turn the volume down on the TV and keep an ear out for what's happening here.

He passes the three of us packets. I flip through mine and see a ton of legal jargon, the words stacked on top of one another in an intimidating mass of print. At the very back there are four lines for signatures. I don't get it. I'm eighteen now – why on earth would they need my parent's permission?

Mr. Graham continues, "We'll start dividing up portions of it immediately, tending to those on the top of donor lists and whatnot. At the same time, we'll continue to study the blood and try to isolate the curative protein within it so that we can replicate it and package it for general consumption. We've already approved the additional research budget. At that time, we'll settle on a price for the cure."

"Price?" I ask, disconcertedly.

"Yes," he replies. "As we speak there are close to forty pharmaceuticals bidding over exclusive access to your blood – I mean, the cure – and the right to patent it for distribution."

"Patent it?" my mother repeats in shock.

"Is that even possible?" Dad asks.

I'm still getting over the fact that he mentioned a price for my blood.

"There are numerous attorneys squabbling over the legalities of this unprecedented situation, Mr. Talloway. What I can assure you is that the FDA has stepped in to create a buffer between your daughter and these companies. No one is getting access to your daughter's blood unless we say so." he states with finality.

"Unless *you* say so," my mother repeats.

My parents look less than pleased.

"What exactly are you asking of us, Mr. Graham?" Dad asks warily.

"Just your continued cooperation," he replies nonchalantly.

"I gather that but...what would your plans require of Nicolette?" Dad clarifies.

"What about school?" Mom jumps in. "Nikki just graduated. She starts at Boston University in less than a month.

"Boston?" The rep's no longer grinning. "Your daughter will be needed on a twenty-four-hour basis. There won't be time for school."

He amends himself at their outraged expressions.

"Please hear me out. What I mean to say is there are certainly a number of decent online schools that could get the job done and allow us to continue with our work."

My parents look even less pleased.

"Mr. Graham..." I ask. "How long would you need me to commit to working with you?"

Mom looks up from the packet. "That's a good question. I didn't even think to ask that."

She looks at Mr. Graham expectantly.

He looks down at his notes, clears his throat and shifts some papers around. I feel a sense of foreboding.

"Um, due to the nature of this work and the gravity of the implications involved, this research period is currently indefinite." He smiles again, trying to win us over. I frown in confusion.

"'Indefinite?'" I ask.

He clears his voice, "For now."

"What the hell does that mean?" Dad asks in disbelief.

"For the rest of her *life*?" Mom gasps.

He winces at her emphasis. I look at him, waiting for a smile or some punch line to indicate that he's joking. The color drains from his face in anxiety.

He's serious.

Indefinitely? How could anyone ask me to commit that amount of time to this...this...project? I could be twenty-eight by the time they're done with me. Thirty five. Fifty. Maybe even seventy! I want to say no. Absolutely not – I refuse to give my life away for their plans. But am I allowed to say no? I have the very thing humankind has been searching for since the beginning of time. The means to cure all disease. No more sickness, no more devastation due to health. How can I withhold something that will help so many lives? This is like organ-donor-benefit on crack! But indefinitely?

Mr. Graham can read our faces.

"Mr. and Mrs. Talloway, the research may not always be indefinite. They may be able to isolate the cure in two years for all we know."

"Or six decades," my father retorts sardonically. Mr. Graham turns a deep shade of crimson.

Dad begins to flip through the packet and his frown deepens as he pauses on a particular page. "Wait a minute…"

Mom looks at him in curiosity. He reads the passage aloud:

"'Mr. and Mrs. Thomas Talloway agree to try and reproduce further progeny for the possibility of another cure source…?'"

"What?!" my mother exclaims.

I hear my siblings bolt up from the couches. The TV might as well be off at this point, it's turned down so low.

They're crazy. Bananas. These people are out of their freakin' minds. My dad slams the packet back on the table.

"What the hell are you doing here?" he growls.

The rep looks very nervous at this point, as if he can see this entire deal falling through right before his eyes. He should be nervous.

"Please. Let's address one thing at a time. We are more than willing to make amendments to this agreement."

"You damn well better be," my dad's voice raises. "You've got a lot of nerve showing up with this garbage!"

"Mr. and Mrs. Talloway, the FDA has many connections. If you work with us, we will more than work with you. We will take care of all of your daughter's financial needs and yours, for that matter. Natalia is still in school, isn't she? Consider her senior year covered. Nathaniel will start college in a year, won't he? Consider his tuition waived. Work with me, and I will make sure you're set for life."

"So now you're trying to buy us?" Mom asks in a taciturn tone. She looks at my Dad and shakes her head. "Unbelievable."

Dad is quiet but I can tell he is furious. He takes a couple of moments to collect himself. Finally, to my surprise, and their credit, they both turn to me.

"Well, Nikki, what do you want to do?"

What do I want to do? How the hell do I answer that? I now have to help people. And it's not that I don't want to. I do.

But at what cost?

And why is there a cost? Why is there a bidding war?

For the past two years, all I've wanted is to go to college: a place where I can have a new slate where nobody knows me and I can start over. Work on my art, talk about novels, and get to know others. Go to a place where I'm being seen.

And loved.

But the realization hits me harder than a lead pipe. With the news of my blood, that college dream will never happen. I may get to go to Boston University and take some cool art classes and learn about Austen and Shakespeare – but I'll never be embraced for being me. Not when the whole world knows that I have something so rare and so wanted.

This sucks. This really sucks.

What do I have to look forward to now?

My next thought jumps to my options. Why is this an either/or scenario? Either give up my life to become their living experiment or lead a life of my own. Why can't I have my cake and eat it too? It's not like I'm asking them to bake it.

"Why can't you guys study my blood during my school breaks?" I suggest.

Mr. Graham looks horrified. He shakes his head vehemently.

"Surely, you must be kidding," he states irritably.

Seriously?

Okay, this is where I draw the line. I may not know exactly what I want but I do know what I *don't* want.

"Funny, I was meaning to ask you the same thing," I snap back. "While you guys were sticking IVs in me left and right, consulting my parents, and talking over my head, I did some serious thinking and this is what I want. I want to help people. But not for a price. I don't care what sort of bidding war is going on – if the goal is to heal people, let's heal people – but not for a pot of gold. Also, this can't take over my life."

I haven't even finished my sentence before he turns to my parents like he didn't even hear me.

"Mr. and Mrs. Talloway –"

"Excuse me? I'm talking to you. In case you've forgotten," I point out, heat rising to my face, "I'm 18-years-old. Regardless of what my parents say, the final decision rests with me. So I suggest you stop ignoring me and listen to what I have to say."

Wow.

I didn't even know I had it in me to stand up for myself like that. My dad tries to hide a smirk of approval. My mom raises an eyebrow in amusement. Mr. Graham, however, is not amused. For the briefest second, a nasty expression of contempt crosses his face, but he recovers, masks it with a strained smile and looks down at his papers, regaining composure.

"Forgive me, Miss Talloway," he says in a controlled, albeit insincere, voice. "You are correct in that the final decision is yours. You are *legally* an adult," – I catch the veiled insult – "and thus you have the freedom and power to help billions of people."

This guy does not play fair.

"I must be honest with you in stating that my superiors insist on the indefinite period of research and development. And they do so with good reason." He leans forward and clasps his hands in front of him. "We do not want to waste time to getting this cure out to the public. Nor do we want to commit to a time frame that may not be fruitful and lose you before the completion of our research."

"They will work as hard and diligently as possible but because of the extraordinary nature of your blood, they have no idea how long it may take to crack the code." He pauses for effect. "Miss Talloway, as we speak, millions of people are dying from all sorts of disease. Do you know how frustrating that is when the cure is sitting right in front of me?" He gestures to me.

My mother leans forward. "We understand your frustration, Mr. Graham. That being said, my daughter is more than the blood running through her veins."

I look at her in surprise. She glances at me and smiles. Thank God someone in this room gets it.

"I want to help you, Mr. Graham," I restate. "But this can't take over my life." He frowns in distaste and shakes his head.

"Forgive me for being blunt, Nicolette, but do you realize how selfish you're being right now?"

Oh, no he didn't! He knocks the breath out of me. My mouth hangs ajar, I'm so speechless.

But my parents aren't.

"That is enough, Mr. Graham," Mom snaps. I don't think I've ever seen her so livid.

My father stands, "I think we're done here."

Mr. Graham opens his mouth as if to say something, looks between my parents and closes it again. Heat rises to his face as he stands and gathers his papers. He wordlessly takes out a business card and slides it across the table at us.

He nods at us and curtly says, "Until next time."

"Don't count on it," Dad snaps.

When the front door closes, Mom lets out a sigh of relief, snatches the business card and tears it into shreds.

"Wretched man."

CHAPTER FIVE

Nicolette:

They really can't take no for an answer. It's been two days since our meeting with Mr. Graham. We've all been holed up in this house and it's starting to strain everyone's nerves – particularly Mom's. We're all walking on eggshells around her. Most of the time she's either deep in discussion with Dad or pacing around the dining room, cell phone in hand. If we happen to startle her or add to her stress, she snaps.

Dad deals with his attorney and forwards all outside inquiries to him. I try to stay distracted. I've read through all of the Jane Austen cannon twice. Now I'm halfway through *Jane Eyre*. Natalia and Nathaniel are on their twelfth movie. When they're not watching a movie, they're busy fighting over which one to watch.

To Natalia's credit, she hasn't once approached me for an interview or comment about this situation. Every now and then I can see the journalist flare in her eyes but she restrains herself. It's probably different too, considering she's a part of the world's latest news story. Dad enters the living room. There's a strange look coloring his expression.

"Nikki," he says. "We…we have another meeting tonight."

"I thought we weren't talking to Mr. Graham or anyone from the FDA." I frown.

"It's not them," he replies. "The President wants to talk to us."

"The *President?*" Natalia repeats. "President Brooklyn Carter? *Our* president?"

I search his eyes. He's serious. Holy shit.

This is so surreal. I'm sitting at my mother's rarely-used formal dining room table, sipping coffee with the most powerful leader in the free world. President Brooklyn Carter. She's an averaged-height woman with thick auburn hair and intelligent brown eyes. She's attractive enough to win votes but not too attractive to repel them. Dressed in a navy blue, well-tailored suit and starched white shirt, her appearance radiates economy and efficiency.

She's been warm and friendly the entire visit, making enough small talk to keep my parents relaxed but staying focused enough to keep my attention. She took pictures with my brother and even answered a few of my sister's burning questions. Now we're alone. One secret service agent stands in the corner of the room. There are at least a dozen spread throughout the property. But for all intents and purposes, this meeting involves just the four of us. She smiles a warm smile and clasps her hands in front of her.

"Mr. and Mrs. Talloway," she looks at me and smiles. "Nicolette. I want to thank you for taking the time to accommodate my visit to your home. It has been a pleasure getting to know you."

What an odd statement, considering the fact that she took the time to fly across the country on Air Force One and meet us in our home; and she's acting like we did *her* the favor. She pauses, searching for words.

"Yesterday morning I received a call from Dr. Richter Shaw, Commissioner of the Food and Drug Administration. I was concerned to hear reports of an agreement falling through at the hands of Mr. Spencer Graham."

"Wretched man," Mom repeats.

"Stacy!" Dad admonishes. He glances at the President apologetically.

"Oh, don't worry Mr. Talloway," President Carter says reassuringly. "I'm not the Gestapo. We are in a free country and you and your wife," she glances at me, "and daughter, are free to criticize whomever you like. Including me."

Dad visibly relaxes. President Carter continues:

"I am sorry to hear of the negative experience you have had with the FDA so far. It is my hope that they have conducted themselves respectfully and that you didn't emerge from the encounter feeling harassed." She looks at us questioningly.

I speak up. "Mr. Graham wasn't willing to work with us – with me. He insisted that the time frame for the research remain indefinite. I'm not willing to commit to something in which I see no end." She nods understandingly. I like her. I was too young to vote for her when she ran three years ago but my parents supported her.

"Nicolette," she begins. "How much time are you willing to commit to this research?" Good question. One I had been thinking about for the past two days.

I look down at my hands. "I am willing to donate as much as I can prior to starting at BU. I'm also willing to donate on a regular basis while I'm studying – so long as it doesn't disrupt my time at BU." I stop and take a deep breath. "I would like to re-assess my willingness to be researched indefinitely once I graduate from college."

"And how much do you expect for your donation?" a brisk voice asks across from me. I look up in surprise. The tone of her voice is very different. I almost think it didn't come from her. I glance at my parents and they too look surprised.

She looks at me unflinchingly and I change my mind. I don't think I like this woman after all.

"Nothing!" I respond in exasperation. Why does everyone think I expect money for my blood?

"Nicolette, I know what it's like to miss college. I had to take a year off to help my mother battle emphysema when I was an undergrad." She gives me a sobering look. "There is honor in sacrifice."

"There's also dignity in compromise." Her eyebrows shoot up in surprise. "I'm sorry but I just want to live as normal a life as I can. I want to help people but I don't want money to be involved. I've told you what I can offer. I've already done one year of living like a lab rat. I can't do another one – especially if there's no end in sight."

A cool look of understanding crosses her face. She leans back in her chair and takes a deep breath, quietly assessing me. Something between a small smirk and smile flashes on her face, she nods and quietly stands. She wordlessly shakes Mom and Dad's hands and nods at me before leaving.

It's been almost a week since our meeting with President Carter. Some things have returned to normal. The press has begun to recede in number and the National Guard left the premises two days ago. Nathaniel has been able to hang out with friends and Natalia plans on moving back into her apartment closer to UW's campus in the next week. I want to feel happy. Like things are finally going back to normal.

But I notice the little things.

Mom and Dad still haven't gone back to work. And they're both constantly on the phone. When they're not held up in a conversation, they have their heads together, making sure to speak softly enough so that no one can overhear them. They've talked to my brother and sister individually and it feels like their doing something. Planning something but I have no idea what. It's dinnertime now and we all gather around the large oak dining table.

"For a while, I thought things would never be the same," I remark quietly. I usually keep quiet during dinners but I feel like I've found my voice. Something about facing off with the FDA and then the President of the United States does a little bit of good for your confidence.

"Tell me about it," Nathaniel replies. "So this is what it feels like to be a celebrity. Um, I think I'll pass." My family laughs at the quip. Mom turns to Natalia.

"Hey, at least you got something out of it," she points out. "Not every junior in college can say they've interviewed the President of the United States."

Natalia jokingly bows to the applause of my brother and dad. "Thank you, thank you. I daresay that was something I planned on accomplishing in my thirties, not at twenty!"

Yeah, things are pretty much back to normal. After dinner, we all say goodnight and head to our rooms. I tuck myself into my bed, pull the covers over and around my ears, and dig my nose into my soft pillow, thankful that the nightmare is over.

BOOM! A thunderous sound erupts from below. The whole house shakes in the vibration. I jolt awake in horror.

"Freeze! FBI!"

No. This can't be happening.

But it is. I pinch myself and stand to my feet as the realization slowly washes over me that the loud sound I heard was the front door being knocked down. I hear several feet disperse at the landing of the house. I jump out of bed and open my door to peek in the hallway.

My Dad suddenly appears before me. I can barely make out his face in the dark, but I can hear in his voice that he's alarmed.

"Get back inside," he orders. "Lock your door."

There's a shiny silver object in his hand, by his side. Oh my God. It's a pistol. He firmly shuts my door before I can say anything else.

I scramble around in my room, my eyes adjusting to the darkness. I slip on a pair of jeans, a hoodie and some sneakers. Yank my cell phone off its charger and shove it in my pocket. The voices below are getting louder... they intermingle with my parents and I can tell things are getting heated.

"Mr. Talloway, I am under strict orders-"

"Get off of my property *now*!"

"Mr. Talloway-"

"You can't have her! What part of that don't you understand?"

"Sir, I am warning you to step aside!"

…The voices grow louder and louder then – BAM! The crack of a pistol erupts in the air, followed by my mother's scream. Feet suddenly disperse and my stomach falls to the soles of my feet. Panic arises in its place.

Someone turns the knob of my door and I suddenly remember I forgot to lock it like Dad said. My door bursts open and I repress the urge to scream. It's my sister, with a tote bag and backpack in hand. Nathaniel runs in behind.

"We have to get out of here," she whispers urgently. There's a cold efficiency in her eyes. She climbs onto my bed and opens the window. She kicks through the screen door and peeks outside.

"Follow me," she whispers.

This is insane.

My bedroom window is elevated roughly twenty to thirty feet from the ground. If any of us fall, we're done. My sister scales the window sill, reaches over to a pipe lining down the side of the house and traverses down the house like an expert mountain climber. She runs out of climbing space about five feet above the ground and jumps.

The voices below grow louder – more aggressive. Nate looks at me.

"Your turn, sis."

I climb through the window with painstakingly careful steps, my chest facing the house. *Oh my God.* I cling to the brick facing of the house and try my best not to look down. Once I reach the pipe, my fear subsides and I'm able to scale down the wall relatively easy. Nate does the same in what seems like five seconds. Show off.

He joins my sister and I on the ground, stomachs flat, as we crawl through the dark terrain of our backyard. Right as we reach the end of the yard, we hear the crack of a pistol. Only this time there's a peal of bullets rung in response. There's no questioning what we just heard. It was the sound of an automatic rifle. There are voices still shouting in the distance but we can't hear our parents' voices anymore.

That's it.

We run.

There's a forest just beyond the perimeter of our yard and we run right into it. Natalia takes the lead, weaving and dodging between trees and branches. The shouting begins to carry outside of the house. They know we're no longer inside. Natalia suddenly stops at a nearby tree. Nate and I screech to a halt beside her, all three of us panting for breath.

"They're dead," she says. We all know who she's referring to. We look at each other as the information tries to sink in but it can't. Not now. Just hours ago, we were saying goodnight. Just minutes ago, Dad was standing at my door.

"We have to split up," Natalia continues. "We have to split up or they'll catch us." She turns to me. "They're not after us, Nikki."

I nod in understanding. My sister shrugs off the backpack and gives it to me. "Mom and Dad wanted us to be prepared. This is for you."

She looks at me for a long moment.

"This isn't your fault," she says quietly.

I nod. She gives me a quick hug and steps back.

Nate wraps me in a strong and tight hug.

"Take care of yourself," he whispers.

"You too."

A dog barks way too close for comfort. Natalia grabs Nathaniel's hand and they run for it. I head in the opposite direction, a deep part of me wondering if I'll ever see my siblings again.

I run. I run as hard as I can in the middle of the forest, cell phone pasted to my ear. I run so hard my chest feels like an inferno. I ignore the burn.

It's the dead of night, and I can hear shouting in the distance pierced every now and then by the dogs barking.

"Information. How can I help you?" the operator asks.

"I need the address for 206-555-6484. Hurry, please!"

Flashlights circle behind me, and I try to run even faster. Suddenly, I lose my footing and trip over an unseen root, cell phone flying out of my hand. I gasp as a shot of pain strikes up through my left ankle. I get back up and scramble to find the phone. There is no time for pain, barely time for running.

"1504 Menlee Drive," the operator rattles off. I shut the phone and take off again. I know the neighborhood he's in. If I can just find the right house.

My race leads me to a residential area. I squint at the little numbers on the street curbs until I find the house I'm looking for and bang on the door. A tall, very young, blonde hair, blue-eyed man opens it.

Jason.

He takes one look at me and wordlessly lets me in.

Brooklyn:

I stride into the opulent office. An anxious pair of feet shuffles behind me. Kennedy Taylor, White House Chief of Staff, briefs me on the situation at hand.

"Her parents wouldn't budge," Kennedy explains. "We had no choice but to take them out."

"Have you forgotten who ordered the hit? The parents are out of the way - good. What about the girl?" I ask sharply. She's the only thing I need.

"Missing." He looks down at his feet. "Her siblings too."

"Jesus, Kennedy!"

"Madame President-"

He stops when I put my hand up.

I sit down at the desk and put my head in my hands. How did an opportunity so brilliant land in my lap only to slip away? It shouldn't have been difficult. Kill the parents, get the girl and secure the cure. Instead, I have a dead set of parents, missing children, and the cure is God-only-knows-where. For the first time in two years, I'm once again struck by the reality that no other woman has sat in this chair. No other woman has led this country. No other President has had this opportunity.

I look down at the papers on my desk. Offers from across the globe lay at my fingers.

China: National debt cancelled.

Saudi Arabia: 50% off oil for five years.

North Korea: Tentative treaty.

Japan: 75% price reduction on imported technology.

All of this in exchange for this girl's blood. The things I can do for this country. The things that will mark my place in history as the first female Commander-in-Chief.

This is an opportunity.

"Find her," I order.

I am not going to miss it.

Jason:

"What happened?"

She's limping. I sit Nicolette down on the nearest sofa and let her catch her breath. I look down at her, and all I can think of is how awful she looks. There's dirt and grass all over her jeans. She's staring into space with a shell-shocked look on her face. I gently take off her shoes – both of them caked with mud. I take off her backpack and give her a blanket to wrap around herself. Then I examine her left ankle. It's already swelling and I can tell it's tender to the touch.

"They're dead," she says in somber disbelief.

"Who?" I ask, still confused. I check for broken bone before wrapping it with an ace wrap. She sprained her ankle.

"My parents."

My eyes snap up to her face.

"They're dead."

A barrage of questions fills my mind, like a flood bursting through a dam, but I don't want to drown her in them. I carry her up to the guest bedroom and try to ignore how right she feels in my arms. She keeps silent from that point on. I sit her on the guest bed.

"They'll recognize you," I say. She remains silent.

It's almost as if she knows what has to be done and lets me do it without raising a single question.

I cut her hair then bleach it blonde with a bottle of peroxide. I give her a spare set of pajamas for the night. Bring her some tea and a couple of Ibuprofens.

"You'll be safe here for the night," I whisper.

We'll figure out the rest tomorrow.

CHAPTER SIX

Nicolette:

I can feel the warm rays hit my face before I open my eyes to see them. I stir in the bed and stretch out my frame. A groan escapes me involuntarily. My left ankle is sore. So are my legs, arms, neck and lower back. Then it hits me. I'm not in my bed. I'm in Jason's house.

Last night really happened.

My parents. My parents are really dead.

Any peace I had in the last few minutes disappear from sight. Sleep time is over – my temporary reprieve is gone. I can't quite describe what it feels like to know that the people who brought you into this world, the people who looked over you and guided you as a shield – the people who were always your safety net – are dead. Gone. I can't ask my mom a question or tell my dad about a concern. They don't have opinions anymore. Their voices are silenced. There is nothing they can do.

They're dead.

And I'm all alone now.

I roll out of bed and stand with shaky legs. Jason's house is one-third the size of mine but it is lovely. Small and cozy with sunlight flooding through every window to every corner of the home, the house is furnished with simple caramel colored woods. The walls are a mix of gold and yellow and something tells me he hired an interior decorator to do the job. I go downstairs, holding the rails, careful not to put too much weight on my left ankle. Something else feels off but I can't quite put my finger on it until I reach the end of the stairs. My hair is gone.

There's not as much weight on my shoulders or head and the back of my neck is bare to the air. I reach up and feel the short, spiky locks, wishing I had a mirror. I'm not going back upstairs so I shrug off the thought and keep walking.

I find him in the kitchen, back facing me as he cooks something on the stove. He must be a morning person. His hair is wet from the shower and he's already dressed in a long gray sweater and khaki pants. His white lab coat hangs on the back of a dining room chair. He must feel my presence because he suddenly turns to me. His eyes are kind.

"Morning," he says in a gentle voice. "How'd you sleep?"

"Okay…thanks." He nods once and looks me over. I can't tell what he's thinking. He turns back to the stove, grabs a plate from a cabinet and dishes the contents of the skillet onto the plate. He puts the plate on the table and pulls a chair out for me in invitation.

"Eggs, sausage, cantaloupe and strawberries. *Bon appétit.*"

"Wow." I sit at the table and scoot in. "Thank you."

He dishes himself a plate and sits across from me.

"No problem."

I dig right in but stop when I see him bow his head. He's praying. I wait for him to finish. I don't want to be rude. He raises his head after a few seconds and I start eating again. The warm eggs fill my mouth and the cool cantaloupes quench my thirst. We're both quiet for a few minutes and I like it. I appreciate it when people don't feel the need to fill in every empty space with words. He doesn't mix his foods. Starts with the sausages, moves on to the eggs and finishes with the fruit. He eats like a doctor. Methodical. He catches me staring and smiles. I suddenly feel warm all over.

"How's your ankle?" he asks.

"It feels better. Still a little sore."

He nods. "You'll have to ice it on and off for a day or two."

"Okay."

He looks down at his hands then back up at me.

"Tell me what happened."

I don't know how long it takes to recount everything. Doing so makes the situation sink in even deeper. The reality that my parents are gone. That there was an act of aggression so vile, so unexpected and it was all for my blood. He listens carefully, interjecting every now and then with a soft question. When I finish, he looks at me with eyes full of something I'm not quite used to. Compassion.

"How are you?" he asks again. "*Really.* How are you?"

I look away from him and fix my eyes on the painting above his fireplace mantle. My nose starts to prickle and tears start to well. I fight to hold them back.

"I can't believe they're gone," my voice cracks.

He reaches his hand across the table and covers mine. I can almost hear him willing me to look at him. When I do, he squeezes my hand and softly says, "I'm glad you came here. I'm glad you trusted me."

I nod silently and a tear escapes, rolling down my right cheek. I swipe it away and am grateful when he doesn't say anything about it. *He gets me.* He understands me in a way that no one ever has before.

Instead of saying anything, he looks at his watch and stands up, gathering his plate and dumping it in the sink. He leans against one of the counters, his eyebrows stitched in thought.

After a while, he says, "You can't stay here."

What does that mean?

He must see the concern on my face because he quickly backs it up with, "No, I didn't mean it like that. I'm glad you came here. I'm saying we have to move. You're not safe here."

It suddenly clicks and I get what he's saying. It doesn't escape me that he said "*we* have to move". Maybe I'm not on my own, after all. I finish my breakfast and pass him the plate.

"I'll get dressed now."

We pull up to what looks like an abandoned boarding house. The building is in horrible shape and the neighborhood is not one I would dare explore at night. Maybe not even during the day. Jason and I are totally out of place in his slick silver Audi. Probably the only two white people on the block.

But Jason seems to feel at ease, even at home, in this depressing gray city. He tells me to stay in the car and then runs up the steps to the dilapidated townhouse. He knocks rapidly, looking around. The reality of my situation sinks in deeper. My parents are gone, my siblings are missing, and I'm currently on the run from the feds. For all we know, they could be watching me with a high powered telescope, waiting to zero in on me. And I hate that this thought isn't so paranoid but actually pretty reasonable considering what happened last night.

A stout black man with cafe-au-lait skin and freckles answers the door in a grandpa sweater. Jason towers over him like he does everyone else. He gives him a brief hug then turns and gestures for me to come in. I pull my backpack and run over to the pair. They quickly usher me inside.

While the outside of the place looks decayed, the inside is warm and inviting with colors of peach and gold accented along the antique wall paper and tables. A staircase meets us at the entrance but to the left of it is a long dark hallway where I'm guessing the rest of the living space is. Jason introduces me.

"Eugene Washington, meet Nicolette Talloway. Nicolette, this is Mr. Eugene Washington, senior director of the Harvest Hope Baptist Shelter."

Mr. Washington gives me a warm smile and shakes my hand.

"Nice to meet you, Nicolette."

"Nice to meet you too," I reply.

Jason explains, "I talked to Mr. Washington last night. He and the folks at the shelter will keep you here today as a favor to me. I have to see what's going on at the hospital and what exactly they want from you."

I look at him in surprise.

"You mean you don't know?"

He shakes his head. "No. Greg – Dr. McGrath - said he would update me but I haven't heard from him in over a week." He must be a mind reader because he answers my top concern. "I'll steer clear of Norris."

"Be careful, Jason."

He smiles. "You too."

He gives Mr. Washington another hug.

"We'll take care of her," he says in assurance.

"Thank you," Jason replies. He gives me another smile then takes off.

"Nicolette, have you eaten?" Mr. Washington asks me.

"Yes, thank you."

"Good," he replies. "Well the staff and residents are still eating in the dining hall. Why don't we take you down there anyway so you can meet the rest of the crew?"

He escorts me to the dining hall: a medium-sized kitchen with a large dining room adjoined. He introduces me to the crew seated around the long oak table: Shawnice, Dayjean, Kim, Carma, Jack, and Isaiah. Carma and Jack are staff members of the shelter. The rest are residents of it. Before Mr. Washington can finish his introductions, a small spat takes place right in front of us.

"Little boy," Shawnice begins. "If you touch my hair one more time, it's off and poppin.'"

I have no idea what she just said but I wouldn't mess with her if I were him. Shawnice is a tall slender black girl with shoulder length braids and what seems like a fiery temperament. She's really pretty and it's easy to see why Dayjean is teasing her. He's a couple shades lighter than her cinnamon complexion and has his hair close cropped with a cool design of the peace sign on the right side. His eyes look like liquid caramel and they dance with laughter as he reaches to touch her hair again.

"Dayjean, leave that girl alone!" a plump black woman with gray curls admonishes the teenager.

Dayjean stops immediately.

Everything about Carma screams maternal – an interesting combination of comfort and fear-inducing respect.

"Carma, they in love." Jack is an elderly dark-skinned man with a rim of gray hair in the back of his bald head. He's very tall and very thin and moves slowly. He ignores the protests of Shawnice and Dayjean and continues with, "Let the youngin's sort it out."

"D, maybe she would give you a chance if you'd stop acting like a damn fool," Kim pipes up and gives Shawnice a high five. She too is a very pretty girl with dark skin and a ponytail slicked back off her face.

Isaiah, a huge, muscular black man nods in agreement. "Exactly. Women don't like brutes, they like gentlemen."

Dayjean puts his hands up in defense.

"Okay, when did this become 'gang-up-on-Dayjean-day?'"

The conversation descends into a mass of multiple voices talking over each other before Mr. Washington whistles for everyone's attention. The voices level off and they turn to face him again.

"Like I was saying," he resumes. "Nicolette is our newest guest. I trust you'll make her feel nice and welcome."

With that, he squeezes my shoulder and heads to his office.

Great.

Now all eyes are on me. I nod and smile nervously. Isaiah gets up and offers me his seat.

"Oh! No, please –"

"It's no problem," he says. "I'll grab another one."

And off he goes. Kim pats the empty seat beside her and gives me a welcoming smile. I take a seat and look down at the plate before me. I can still feel everyone's eyes on me and I feel completely out of place. This is going to sound totally white (and probably messed up) but I've never been in an environment where I was the only white person in the room. In fact, I've never been in an environment where I was a part of the minority. I'm so used to seeing other people – most people – look and act like me, I might as well have green skin for all the discomfort I'm feeling right now. Is this what people of color feel like on a day-to-day basis?

A soft maternal voice floats over to me.

"Did you have anything to eat, baby?" Carma asks. How can a question be so comforting? An endearment so inviting? And from a stranger no less!

"Yes, thank you." I quietly reply. She grabs an empty bowl and pours some oatmeal before passing it to me.

"Well, eat some more." she says. "You look as thin as a rail."

"Carma!" Shawnice exclaims in surprise.

"What?" she asks in confusion. "She does!"

It's okay. I'm not offended. On the contrary, I'm very amused by her honesty. She handles feeding me like it's a battle mission and she's the general in charge.

"Dayjean, wash your hands and go get her some tea." she orders.

"And some napkins," Jack adds.

"And some toast," Kim contributes. I smile at Dayjean apologetically. He rolls his eyes in good humor and goes to the kitchen.

"So where are you from, Nicolette?" Shawnice asks.

"Um, Clyde Hill." I reply.

Dayjean returns with the goods and hands them to me. He flicks Shawnice's braid as he sits down.

"Clyde Hill, huh? That's a long way off. How'd you hear about us?" he asks.

"I didn't," I respond. "Jason brought me here."

The whole group perks up at the sound of his name. I swear Carma just grew three inches.

"Jason?" Kim exclaims.

"My baby!" Carma squeals.

"Jason brought you here?" Kim asks. "How is he?"

"Well –"

"He didn't even stop to say hello," Carma frowns. "Oh, he's in trouble now. Just way 'till I see that boy!"

"Carma, leave that chile alone!" Jack responds.

I defend him. "He – he was in a rush. He had to get to work but he'll be back this afternoon."

This placates her a bit. Carma leans back in her chair and drops the protest.

Isaiah finally enters the room with a small office chair in tow. "*Doctor* Jason Monroe. He's done us something proud."

Jack nods in agreement. "Indeed. Yes, indeed."

"DAYJEAN!" We all jump at the sound and turn in time to see Shawnice pick up her empty plate and smack Dayjean on the back of his head with a loud clang. His hands fly to his head as he bends over with an expression of mingled pain and shock.

Carma gives a huge crack of a laugh, her whole body jiggling on jovial giggles. She sounds like something between a hyena and Tigger from *Winnie the Pooh*. To my surprise, everyone else at the table joins in her laughter.

She points at Dayjean and says in between breathes of sniggling humor, "That's what yo' dumbass gets! I done told you to leave that baby alone. Whoo-hoo-hoo!"

She gives Shawnice a high five. Shawnice catches me staring and throws me a mischievous wink. And for the first time in almost twenty four hours, I smile.

After breakfast, Carma takes me to a small, old wood-paneled guest room and practically orders me to take a nap. When she closes the door, I sit on the creaky bed and look around. I appreciate the chance to gather my thoughts and be alone. I pull out the backpack Natalia gave me. I didn't have the chance to look through it last night or this morning. Now, I can see what she packed for me.

I unzip the bag and find clothes and toiletries neatly packed and stuffed at the top. I pull them out and to my surprise and delight, I find two of my favorite books inside: *Persuasion* and *North & South*. I pull them out and lay them beside the clothes. The bag isn't empty yet.

I pull out an envelope that reads "Last Will and Testament" on the front. I place it aside, reach in again and this time feel cash. Wads and wads of it, lining the bottom and sides of the backpack, held by numerous rubber bands. I flip the bag over and in an instant half of my bed is covered by a mountain of dollar bills. Every visible wad is stacked with hundreds of dollars. I count out one of the wads then two. Each of them has twenty hundred-dollar bills intact. If all of these wads carry the same amount, I could easily have over $50,000 sitting on my bed. Something slips off my bed and falls to the floor with a loud clank. I reach down to pick it up and find a frame. Inside, there's a small, worn picture of my family in the backyard smiling for the camera. I couldn't have been any older than five.

I squeeze the back of the frame and notice that it feels padded. I flip the frame around, remove the backing of it and find what is stuffed behind. Tucked in the back of the frame is a small envelope with my name written across it. It's my mother's handwriting. I tear it open and unfold the two sheets enclosed – both covered with her neat and elegant script.

Dear Nicolette,

My second treasure. The quietest of the group. I find it so ironic that the most reserved of my children would end up with the most attention worldwide. If you are reading this, dear daughter of mine, then I am no longer with you. Your father and I decided to make some preparations in case things did not go as we hoped. Enclosed are some emergency funds.

$180,000 divided evenly between you, your brother and your sister. There are more funds available at an offshore account accessible by the codes written in our last will and testament (you'll find that enclosed as well).

I stop reading for a moment. They knew. They knew something was wrong and they prepared for the worst. I don't know if I should be glad or furious. Grateful or devastated. They knew they were going to die. Or at least that it was a possibility. Because of me.

For me.

A tear slips out of my eye, down my cheek, and past my chin. I can taste the salty water on my tongue. I swipe away the tears and dig my fingers into the soft spikes of my short hair. I look back down at the letter. It's like my mother read my thoughts before I even thought them:

We want you to know that none of this is your fault. Nikki, we are so proud of you for how you've handled such a profoundly burdensome gift. We are amazed at your maturity and clarity of thought. And yet somehow I knew you would be able to take this situation in stride. You are our youngest daughter. Your father and I have often wondered if we should have pushed you more to share your heart. Please know that our silence in the midst of your silence did not come from a place of disinterest. We came to accept that this is how you were made: to be quieter than the rest and we didn't want to push you or assume that your reserved nature came from a place of trauma. I hope we were right in doing so.

If you are reading this letter – and I hope to God that you are not – then this is all we can do for you. We love you. We always have and we always will. We want you to do what is best for you. So do it.

Love,
Mom and Dad

I don't know how long I cry but I try my best to keep my sobs as quiet as possible. No one is there to see the tears. No one is there to dry them. In the tiny corner of Harvest Hope Baptist Shelter, I finally allow myself to grieve the loss of my parents.

CHAPTER SEVEN

Brooklyn:

"What do we do with the bodies?" Kennedy asks.

"Bury them in an unmarked grave. The last thing we need is grave robbers."

"Together?" he asks.

"Well, they *were* married!" I snap. He nods. I call Elizabeth Shune, Press Secretary, and arrange for a press release.

"Focus on the girl. Our efforts to find her. Make it seem like we're on her side," I instruct her. "Call it self-defense. Their deaths were an unfortunate accident that happened in the heat of the moment. I want the speech two hours before I make the address. Don't forget, Ms. Shune, the FBI acted out of self defense," I repeat to her. I hang up and catch Kennedy watching me in inquiry.

"Kennedy, if the public finds out that I ordered a hit on Nicolette Talloway's parents, they'll be screaming for *my* blood – not hers. I don't want us to come across as the aggressors. As far as America knows, we are a concerned party intervening for the well-being of an 18-year-old girl who is now an orphan. Got it?"

He nods again and leaves the office. I lean back in my plush leather chair and remind myself that there are only so many places she can be. We caught her off guard. She couldn't have gotten very far.

I pick up the phone again.

"Casey, get Agent Dannican in here. I want a briefing on the search."

Jason:

I've only been here a couple of hours but my stomach is in knots. I can't believe I forgot that Greg doesn't come on shift until noon. Today is his half-day sabbatical. I try to keep normal, go on my rounds, check in with patients, giving clearance to some and recommendations to others. When I finish with my patients, I head over to my office to do some busy work. Maybe I can settle my nerves there. As I pass the nurse's station, I notice today's paper. Nicolette's high school picture is on the cover. The headline reads: "NICOLETTE TALLOWAY – GIRL WITH THE BLOOD CURE – MISSING".

How original.

I make it to my office but when I'm there, I can't sit still. I can't talk to any of the nurses, none of the other doctors on staff. Greg McGrath is the only one I can trust. Someone knocks on the door and I jump in surprise. I barrel over to it, trying to keep a poker face.

Thankfully, it's Greg.

I let him in soundlessly and he begins to pace instead of me.

"I came here as soon as I could," he starts. "I was going to call you but I guess you already heard."

"Greg, I need to talk to you."

"Jason, I'm sorry. She's missing. The feds tried to grab her but they screwed up."

"Greg –"

"Norris insisted that we do the press release. I knew better than to-"

"Greg, I know where she is."

He stops in his tracks.

"What?"

I lower my voice. "She came to my place last night."

He frowns in confusion. "How did she –"

"I don't know," I answer. "Somehow she found me. You should have seen her, Greg. She looked like hell."

He looks down at his feet, brows furrowed in thought.

"Greg, her parents are dead."

His head snaps back up. "Christ, Jason! Is she still at your place now?"

"No," I shake my head. "I took her somewhere safe."

"Where?"

I shake my head again. "It doesn't matter. She's safe for now."

"Jason, the public doesn't know all the details. All they know is that she's missing."

"I know," I reply.

"What about her siblings?" he asks, almost as an afterthought.

"Missing too."

His eyebrows shoot up in surprise. He runs his hand through his hair and holds it at the crown.

"Listen, Jason. I have a family to take care of. I don't want to get involved in this-"

"Of course," I cut in. "I would never ask you to do anything to jeopardize the safety of your kids! I'm off duty at the lab for a couple of weeks. I need time off here too."

"Why?" His eyes crease in confusion.

"I have to help her."

"Are you out of your mind?" he exclaims. He lowers his voice and continues with, "Jason, the feds are after this girl. If you get involved, you become an accessory to a fugitive!"

"But why is she a fugitive?" I retort. "She's done nothing wrong! These people have murdered her parents, scattered her siblings, and scared her shitless. I have to help her. I'm the only person she trusts."

"Maybe if you turn her in, this whole situation can be diffused."

I shake my head adamantly. "Absolutely not. Not after what they did to her parents. I'm the only person she trusted enough to turn to. I'm not going to betray her and turn her back in."

He sighs and I can tell he's not convinced.

"Look, I'm not asking you to get involved," I reason. "I'm just asking you to give me time off. Once I leave, you can forget I even exist."

"Don't be stupid," he replies. "You have two weeks off as long as you stay in touch with me. Believe it or not, I do actually care if you manage to stay alive or not."

I smile at his sarcasm.

"Thanks, Greg."

"Does Norris know?" he asks.

"No," I reply.

"Good," he nods. "Let's keep it that way."

We shake hands and he leaves the office.

The day carries on as it usually does and I find out that the staff at the hospital are as unaware of the feds' intentions as the staff at the lab. After lunch, I head to the nurse's station to pick up my charts for another set of rounds. I feel a vibrating in my right pocket and pull out my cell phone.

"Hello?"

"Jason? Oh, thank God!" a female voice exclaims on the other end. Her voice is very urgent. "Jason, it's Kim. Get out of there. They're onto you."

"What?" I ask in confusion.

"They're onto you!" Kim insists. "Don't you have the news over there?"

I look at an overhead television playing down the hall in the waiting room. The channel is on CNN and to my horror my face is plastered on the corner of the screen. Next to my picture is footage of several vehicles surrounding my house, federal agents ransacking the interior, searching high and low. The headline beneath the screen reads: NICOLETTE TALLOWAY THOUGHT TO BE ON THE RUN WITH DR. JASON MONROE.

Oh my God.

My heart feels like it's about to pop out of my chest. I hear a faint ringing in my ears and feel really lightheaded.

Snap out of it, Jason! I order myself. I can't faint now.

I look around me and mercifully the nurses and doctors near me haven't noticed the headline yet.

"Jason!" I whip around and catch Greg hightailing it towards me, a panicked look in his eyes. I bring the phone back to my ear.

"Kim, is she okay?" I ask.

"She's fine. We're hiding her. Just get out of there - *now*!"

I shut my phone as Greg reaches me. He reaches for my hand and presses what feels like money in my palm. He pulls me close to him and whispers, "Did you tell anyone else? You're all over the Internet." He looks over my shoulder. "Oh no."

I follow his eyes and see several black vehicles pull up to the entrance of the building. He pulls my shoulders to face him again.

"In the stairwell, there's a map of an old evacuation route. The hospital hasn't used it since the fifties," he whispers. "Go! I'll cover you."

I run into my office, grab my backpack and pour the contents of my desk drawer into it — unlock my office safe and pull out the emergency cash stashed in it. Grab a baseball cap off my desk and shove it into my bag. I turn off my cell phone. The last thing I need is for them to trace me through the GPS in my phone or hear it vibrating as I run.

I open the door and peek out slowly. There is a wall of white lab coats and scrubs holding off the feds, asking questions. Greg is in the front leading the charge. I stay low and run to the stairwell opposite the nurse's station. I close the door as quietly as I can and look around.

The stairwell dark and poorly lit. I run my fingers along the wall and find the map. I can barely make out the route Greg was talking about but I have no choice but to move. I run down the stairs to the bottom of the foundation. Just as I reach the bottom, I hear the stairwell door open above me. Voices quickly follow.

"Penner, take east. Shaunder, west. Close him off!"

"Shit!"

They're literally on top of me. I reach into my lab coat and pull out my penlight. It's not very effective but it helps me make out the antiquated, cob-webbed door that leads to the original evacuation route. I wrench open the old door and step through. A putrid smell more foul than a mortuary assaults my nose. I close the door behind me and move forward; the farther I move, the quieter their voices become.

The inefficient route takes me almost a full hour to navigate but to my relief I finally reach a ladder leading to the top of a drainage sewer. I climb the ladder, twist the lid and pop it open. I raise my head through the opening slowly. Fresh air fills my nostrils. There's no one waiting to cuff me at the opening so I pull myself out of the sewer completely. I stand up and look around. The route has led me to an abandoned alley nearly eight blocks away from the hospital. I've never been so grateful for a complete deviation from my starting point.

I place the lid back on the sewer opening, take off my lab coat, roll it up and shove it into my backpack. I grab the baseball cap I packed earlier and pull it on as close to my eyes as possible. I take the stairwell map and toss it in a nearby dumpster before heading over to the closest subway.

CHAPTER EIGHT

Nicolette:

We're all nervous. Everyone at the shelter tries to act normal, play it off as if everything is fine. But I know they're all concerned. Ever since Kim got off the phone with Jason, we've been anxious to hear how he's doing. For the past five hours, I've been hiding in the attic with an ice pack over my ankle. There's a floorboard opening that I can sneak into if anyone were to search. Isaiah somehow knew what position I needed to be in as well as what coverings I needed to have over me in order to avoid being scented by guard dogs. It's made me more curious about his background and how he knows what he knows.

Fortunately, his expertise wasn't needed today. No one came knocking on our door, searching for me. But Jason isn't home yet. We'd really like to hear his knock.

When it's time for dinner, Carma, or "Mama C" as everyone calls her, convinces Mr. Washington to let me come down and eat with them.

"If anyone busts in, we'll rush her back up. Don't worry!" she assures him. I make my way down to the dining hall, my ankle is pretty much pain-free at this point and the swelling has gone down significantly.

We gather around the modest oak table. The food smells absolutely tantalizing and I can't wait to dig in. But before we eat, we stand in a circle and grab hands. I look around in confusion. If I hadn't seen this in movies, I would have no context for what we're doing. Mama C stands at the head of the table and begins, "Let's thank the Good Lord. Close your eyes, bow your heads."

Everyone obeys.

"Dear Jesus, thank you for this bountiful, merciful feast. Thank you for the hands that made it and the money that provided it. Lord, we also thank you for Nicolette joining us here today. Thank you for bringing such a special jewel into our midst."

Wow. No one has ever called me that.

"Lord, we pray that you will help her in her current situation. We thank you that you have provided humanity with such a gift through her and we ask that you would use her in mighty ways." Several soft utterances of "Mmm-hmm" support her prayer. Just when I think we're done, Isaiah puts in a prayer of his own.

"Father, we lift up Jason to you," he begins. Everyone utters in agreement.

"Lord," he continues. "Please keep him safe and give him guidance as to where he needs to be and what he needs to do. Thank you for his heart and his willingness to help Nicolette. I know that you will reward him for his efforts."

Mama C picks up again, "Please bless this food that we are about to partake in. Let it add to the nourishment of our bodies and bless the fellowship at this table today. We ask this –"

"In Jesus' name. Amen!" Jack finishes impatiently.

"Amen!" The crew echoes. I feel both of my hands squeezed at the same time before we let go.

I open my eyes and lift up my head to see Jack shaking his in irritation. "You and Isaiah ain't prayin' over our food no more," he decides. "Y'all take too damn long. The Lord said 'let us give thanks,' broke bread and did eat. Not 'let us give thanks for a half hour and let the food get cold.' Good God!"

Kim and Shawnice bust out in laughter. Dayjean even claps his hands.

"Jack, hush up and eat your food!" Mama C snaps back.

"Don't mind him, Mama C. He's just grumpy 'cause he's hungry," Kim points out, shoulders bouncing in laughter.

We pass the food around and soon the conversation picks up as we eat. Isaiah is sitting to my right, Kim to my left. Dinner here is completely different than I've ever experienced. For one, the food is incredibly delicious. A southern feast of chicken, macaroni and cheese, collard greens, and homemade biscuits. The conversation is lively and for once in a very long time, I'm intentionally pulled into the discussion. There's no allowance for a wallflower at this table. When the conversation shifts to a topic I can't speak on, I turn to my right.

"Isaiah?" I ask timidly. "Who exactly were you praying to? God or Jesus?"

He cocks his head at me and thinks for a moment.

"They're one and the same," he says. "Have you heard of the trinity?"

I nod.

"Well, God is the Father, the Son – Jesus, and the Holy Spirit. Three in one," he explains.

"I thought there was only one God in Christianity," I say, confused.

"There is," he replies. "Three in one. Think of a family. There are multiple members and individuals in it but the family exists as one unit. Or the human body; it has multiple limbs and organs but it is still one body. So in the same way, God exists as three persons in one. Does that make sense?" He asks.

I nod. Surprisingly it does. I think on what he's told me. Growing up, my family went to church on Christmas or Easter but around the time Natalia left for school, we stopped going altogether. I don't even know if God exists and if he does, what am I supposed to do? Is there a heaven and hell? If there is, how do I get into the former when I die and not the latter? I remember Jason praying over breakfast and I wish he was here so I could ask him. I wish he was here so I'd know he's okay.

I look past Isaiah and catch Carma watching me, a small smile on her face. Could her old ears possibly have caught the conversation from the other end of the table? Or is she a mind reader, able to tell who I was thinking about?

Someone knocks on the door.

Our conversation screeches to a halt and several forks drop to their plates with a small clink. Kim, Carma, and Shawnice look at me in concern. Isaiah and Mr. Washington head down the hall to the door.

"Should we take her up?" Kim whispers.

"Not yet," Carma replies. "They'll let us know if we need to hide her." It feels strange having people talk about me in front of me, like I'm not even in the room. For once, I'm actually grateful for it. It's less overwhelming to have someone else look out for your welfare.

We hear muffled voices near the door, followed by several footsteps making their way back to the dining room. Mr. Washington comes in followed by Isaiah and then...

"Jason!" I gasp. I want to run up and give him a hug but Carma beats me to it.

"My baby!" she exclaims as she squeezes him close to her.

"Hi, Auntie C."

He smiles and hugs her tightly in return. His eyes search the room and land on me. I can see relief wash over his face. When Carma lets him go, she immediately takes off his jacket.

"Shawn," she says, "go fix him a plate."

Shawnice gets to it without a word. Dayjean grabs another chair and parks it next to me. Jason takes the seat and asks me, "You okay?"

I nod. "You?"

He nods.

Shawnice sets a hot plate in front of him. He looks up at her in appreciation, "Thanks, Shawn." He also catches Kim's eye, "Thanks for the tip."

She smiles in response and shakes her head.

"How on earth did you get out of there?" she asks in wonder.

Jason shakes his head, his mouth already full of food. He swallows a bit of it and replies, "Long story. Better question: how did I become their target?"

"That's easy: the dogs," Isaiah says. We all turn to him for more. He looks at me.

"They probably traced Nicolette's scent to your house. You went directly to his place, right?"

I nod. A wave of guilt washes over me.

"I'm so sorry, Jason," I tell him remorsefully.

He shakes his head.

"Uh-uh. None of that. It's not your fault."

"I know it's not," I reply. "But as long as I'm around you, you're at risk." I look up at the crew. "All of you are at risk."

Carma walks up behind me, wraps her big soft arms around me and pulls me into a gentle hug.

"Nonsense, baby," she says. "We hid you here all day and ain't nobody broke in here."

"Yet," I point out.

"Chile, please." Jack pipes up, "This is the last place they gon' check. It's probably why the young man brought you here in the first place."

I shake my head vehemently and stand up. Everyone looks at me, waiting for me to speak. Jason's eyes are fixed on me but I look anywhere but back at him.

"They're going to keep searching." I let that statement sink in. "And when they find out about Jason's ties to this shelter, they're going to come knocking on this door."

"We can handle it," Dayjean says.

"The last time anyone tried to handle the feds in my defense, they ended up dead."

Silence washes over the room.

"I'm not willing to let the same thing happen to you," I whisper.

I can feel Jason's eyes on me, willing me to look at him but I won't. If I do, I might lose my resolve. He clears his throat and finally says, "Okay. We'll leave first thing in the morning."

Now I look at him.

"*I'll* leave first thing in the morning," I reply.

"You're not going without me," he retorts.

"I'll figure this out on my own," I insist.

"How?" he snaps. "You don't have any money, any connections, no car. You don't even have a subway ticket for God's sake!"

"Jason Dockery Monroe!" Carma admonishes.

His face turns red and he takes a deep breath, regaining his composure. He has a point – although he doesn't yet know about all the cash my parents left me. I sit back down and touch his arm, ignoring our captive audience.

"Jason, I couldn't live with myself if what happened to my parents happens to you."

He looks at me and offers a gentle smile.

"And I couldn't live with myself if I didn't help you finish this," he replies. "Nic, if it wasn't for me, you would be with your parents and siblings, living a normal life."

"That's not true-"

"Yes, it is," he insists. "I discovered your blood typing anomaly and I was part of the team that brought attention to it."

"That doesn't mean it's your fault," I reply.

He shakes his head, "Even if it wasn't, I want to help you because I care about you. Because we're friends."

That last sentence hits me like a blast of cold air. *Because we're friends.* I can't remember a time when I considered anyone my friend or vice versa. He's not helping me out of some nostalgic sense of obligation. He's helping me because he's my friend. And he cares. I accept his friendship in one little word.

"Okay."

After dinner, we all disperse to different parts of the house. Shawnice and Kim call it a night. Jason and I stay in the dining room and he tells me how he managed to escape.

"Once I was clear of the hospital, I took the subway and hid in a café on the other side of town, trying to stay low until dark. I figured it would be harder for them to spot and follow me here if I waited until night."

"Why didn't you call?" I ask. But I realize the answer as soon as the question comes out of my mouth.

"I couldn't risk turning on my cell and having them trace me, much less having them trace my call to you and the crew."

I nod in understanding.

"I'm so glad you're okay," I blurt out. I look down in embarrassment and feel my cheeks begin to flush with color. He lifts my chin with the edge of his finger and meets my eyes.

"Ditto," he smiles.

My breath catches and for the first time in over a year, I feel slightly off-kilter in his presence. He's really good-looking and really kind. And I'm probably reading way too much into his kindness but I don't want to drop this moment. His expression sobers and he looks at me intently, leaning closer as if on autopilot. To my surprise and utter approval, I begin to lean closer to him. His eyes shift down and I know he's looking at my lips. He's about to kiss me! I lick my lips and look down at his as we slowly close the space between us until-

"Hey guys, look at this!" Dayjean yells.

We snap back like a pair of rubber bands and look at anything but each other. I get up before Jason can say anything and follow Dayjean into the living room. We all assemble into the room and watch the TV, parked on CNN. The men remain standing but Carma and I sit on the love seat together.

The headline reads: PRESIDENT CARTER MAKES ANNOUNCEMENT REGARDING NICOLETTE TALLOWAY. The President stands in a hallway of the White House, the podium emblazoned with the United States seal. She's in the middle of her speech.

"We are doing everything in our power to find Nicolette – not for our benefit but for her safety," she says.

"Your 'safety?' Are they out of their minds?" Dayjean asks.

She continues with, "It is with great sadness and regret that I must inform you of the deaths of Nicolette's parents, Thomas and Stacy Talloway."

The sentence cuts at me like a pen knife opening a raw scab. Carma squeezes my leg in comfort and I lay my hand over hers.

"On the night of August 12, Agent Michael Dannican and his team sought to gain custody of Nicolette for the sake of her protection. The news of her blood has been released worldwide and it was our concern that such news has placed a high number on her head. Our hope was to protect her from bounty hunters, foreign agents, and other individuals who would seek to sequester her for the value of her blood."

Bounty hunters, foreign agents... I've been so busy trying to deal with my own country, I never stopped to think about the advances of other nations. I feel even less safe now. She continues:

"There was a terrible miscommunication between Agent Dannican and Nicolette's parents," she continues. "Mr. Thomas Talloway ultimately chose to fire at Agent Dannican and Agent Dannican's team acted to protect their leader and their own lives. Their act of self-defense ended with the tragic loss of Mr. and Mrs. Talloway. In the midst of such horrific events, Nicolette and her siblings left the premises, no doubt terrified for their own well-being. I want to stress that at no point were these children in harm's way. Agent Dannican was under strict orders to secure Nicolette in a safe and orderly fashion. Under no circumstance would I allow for a single hair on those children's heads to be harmed."

No, just my parents' heads.

Something between hatred and rage suffuses my senses. Every single word out of this woman's mouth is bull and she's getting away with it. I think back to that night. There was no communication between the feds and my parents. It was their way or the highway. I remember the look of trepidation in Dad's eyes. I can still hear my Mom's screams. If they wanted to protect me, why not just explain that to my parents without breaking down their door? Why didn't she tell them when she met with us in our dining room? If I'm certain of anything, it is this: they did not come to protect me.

My parents were protecting me.

A hand squeezes my shoulder and I jump slightly. I look up to see Jason looking at me, his face creased with concern.

"Are you okay?"

I look around and everyone is watching me. The TV is off. The press conference over. Jack isn't even in the room anymore. I must have zoned out.

"What else did she say?" I ask.

"She said they're going to keep searching," Isaiah answers. "For the sake of your 'safety.'" He rolls his eyes.

"Oh, God." I cover my eyes with both my hands. Carma squeezes me close to her.

"Don't worry, baby. It'll be alright," she assures.

I know she doesn't know how this will turn out but the words and her warm embrace comfort me anyway.

Mr. Washington adds, "They're limiting the search to Washington State right now but she's asked the nation to be vigilant."

"Which is all the more reason we need to leave tomorrow," Jason says.

"You gonna leave the state?" Dayjean asks.

Jason nods.

"How do you know they won't pick you up at a toll station?" Mr. Washington asks.

Jason shrugs. "I don't. But I know we can't stay in the state and wait for them to happen upon us."

He looks down at me and I nod in agreement.

"Where will you go?" Carma asks.

Jason scratches the back of his neck.

"I have a friend in San Diego who might be able to help us. If he can isolate the protein in Nicolette's blood, then this whole search can come to an end."

"They won't need me anymore and I'll be free."

Isaiah nods in agreement.

"Stop at Eva's place on your way there."

"Eva?" Jason frowns. "I thought she was in Turkey?"

Isaiah shakes his head. "She got back two months ago. She's stationed in Yreka, California for now." He gives Jason the most serious look I've ever seen cross his face. "Make sure you stop there. She can really give you a hand."

Jason looks at him for a moment and nods in full understanding. I don't know who this person is or why she's so important but apparently Jason does. And that's enough for me.

Mr. Washington stretches. Dayjean and Mama C follow suit.

"We'd better hit the sack. The earlier you leave, the better," he says.

"Geez, Mr. Washington, when you put it like that..." I tease.

The group bursts in laughter. Who knew I could make people laugh?

"Oh, no, I didn't mean-"

I smile to reassure him that I'm teasing. He smiles in amusement and we all head to bed.

CHAPTER NINE

Nicolette:

We rise early and eat light. Jason checks and re-checks everything we need before we hit the road. Even though the sun hasn't risen, the whole crew is up and willing to help. We all finally make it to the car Jason and I will use. It's an old, red, beat up Camry. I almost laugh at the look on Jason's face.

"Are you sure this thing works?" he asks with a skeptical look. Dayjean steps forward with a nostalgic expression of pride. He pats the roof of the car fondly.

"Oh, yeah." he says. "Cami will never do you wrong. This babe is one-hundred percent reliable."

Kim mentions, "Dayjean just got a new car a few months ago but he used to drive this one like crazy."

"Ever wash it?" Jason asks wryly.

"Hell naw, man! Why should I pay fifteen dollars to wash this car when God will do it for me for free ninety-nine?"

"Did you just say 'free ninety-nine?'" Kim shakes her head.

"And what does God have to do with this?" Isaiah asks in confusion.

"Oh, Lord." Shawnice says. "Here we go again."

Dayjean insists, "God made rain for a reason. He sends it every now and then to wash this baby for me."

My mouth drops.

"You are out of your mind, D." Kim says in amusement.

"Hey, it says it in the Good Book. 'There is a time for everything and a season for every activity under the sun.'" His face takes on a pious expression and he speaks in a stuffy tone, "'A time to be born and a time to die. A time to plant and a time to uproot. A time to love and a time to hate.' A time to give sunshine and a time to wash Dayjean's car. Amen, thank you Jesus." And with that, he nods his head and closes his eyes as if to say "and that's that."

I'm gonna miss these guys.

The thought hits me as quick as a bolt of lightning striking the ground. But it's true – I really am going to miss each and every one of them. I notice Mama C has been conspicuously quiet this whole time. She's still in her pink robe and slippers and has her gray locks in pink curlers. I can tell she's taking our departure hard. Jason looks at his watch and I know he's ready to move. I wordlessly join him in loading the car with our few belongings. Jason and I give each of the crew a hug and say some parting words.

"Thank you. Thank you so much for helping me."

I save Mama C for last and she gives me a parting hug that nearly breaks my ribs but I wouldn't have it any other way.

Jason takes the wheel and backs out of the narrow driveway. We wave goodbye and head off to our new destination, shelter and the crew in the rear view mirror.

Jason:

Both of us are quiet the first couple of hours. We drive by streams and streams of dark evergreen trees. I keep the radio off, just in case a newsreel upsets her. She's sleeping right now, spiked blonde hair resting against the passenger window. I can already see specks of black cropping up in her roots. She looks so peaceful. I want to keep it that way.

I turn down the volume on the GPS Isaiah gave me and let my mind linger on the crew. I knew they would be welcoming but their generosity has blown me away. I know they're not rolling in dough, but they've already given us a car, a GPS, and more than enough food to last us for the trip. I smile as I think of Aunt C's insistence that I pack the dozen pieces of Tupperware leftover she fixed for us.

The route is a fairly straight shoot down the I-5. It takes less than three hours to cross the state line into Oregon. To my relief, the toll person barely glances my way. Takes the money and pushes the button. By the time we reach Portland, Nicolette is up and watching the scenery. I reach behind me for one of the Tupperware.

"You hungry?" I ask. I hand her a box and she digs right in.

"Are we in Oregon now?" she asks.

"Mm-hmm. Salem's coming up soon. Need a bathroom break?"

"No, I'm fine."

"Well, I do." I take the closest exit to a gas station. "Be back in a second." She nods and I dash to the men's room. To my relief, it isn't nearly as filthy as I was steeling myself for.

Neither of us has said anything about this morning. Or what almost happened last night. We have nearly five hours left in this drive and unless she plans to sleep the whole time, I wonder if I should address it and clear the air.

When I'm finished in the restroom, I stride over to the junky red car. Despite my misgivings about it, it's actually pulled through really well for us. To my surprise, the closer I get to the car, the more apparent it is that Nic is not in the passenger seat. She's strapped in at the driver's wheel. I walk up to her side and she rolls down the window.

"What are you doing?" I ask.

"Jason, you've driven almost four straight hours. I'm gonna give you a break." I'm shaking my head vehemently before she even finishes her sentence.

"No," I yank open the driver's side.

"Jason!"

"Shhh!" I warn her, looking around. She immediately quiets. I lower my voice, "Nic, you're the most wanted woman in the world right now. The last thing we need is a cop stopping you for a missed turn signal, asking for your ID and vehicle registration."

Understanding dawns on her face and she silently gets out of the car and re-enters on the passenger side. I look around. Thankfully no one seems to have noticed our little argument. I put the car in gear and merge onto the freeway again. She keeps silent and I look over at her.

"I know you were trying to help. I appreciate it, Nic. I really do."

She runs a hand through her spiky locks.

"I just feel so useless right now."

I wasn't expecting that. Eyes on the road, I reach over and find her hand. I give it a gentle squeeze and say, "You are beautiful, kind, caring and wickedly intelligent. Believe me, you are many things, Nicolette Talloway. Useless is not one of them."

She smiles at me. "Thanks."

I pull my hand away. I knew this would be difficult - spending so much time with her. I could hardly keep it together when we were in the ER over a year ago. And when the research started, I purposefully chose not to work closely with her, if only to avoid whatever feelings are emerging between us. She's so hard to read sometimes. I don't know if she wants me too or if I make her nervous in a "get-away-from-me-you-creep" kind of way.

Pull it together, man.

She has so much to worry about - the last thing she needs is any advance from me. And I don't want her to think I'm only helping her to take advantage of her or to have her owe me in some way. Regardless of what I'm feeling, I need to help her. Protect her.

Even if it's from myself.

Nicolette:

Jason continues to drive down the 5 and I'm struck by the reality that is my new life. No school, no work, no parents and no siblings. It's like my life has narrowed into this tunnel vision of trying to get away and stay ahead of those literally out for my blood. It's just me…and Jason. A guy I never thought would notice me has single-handedly taken my well-being as his responsibility. I'm also struck by the fact that I know so little about Jason. I've been acquainted with him for over a year but I don't really know anything about him or his background.

So I ask him the same question I asked him almost two years ago, "Jason, how old are you?"

He looks at me for a moment. "Twenty-one," he finally says.

Holy crap. So he doesn't just *look* really young. "How on earth are you a licensed doctor at twenty-one?"

"Child prodigy." I look for the joke in his eyes but he's dead serious.

"Tell me," I say.

He takes a deep breath and dives in.

"When I was born, my birth mother abandoned me at the hospital where she gave birth." My eyes widen in shock. "I got bounced around from one foster home to another. Most good, some bad. When I was eight, I ended up with a nurse named Caroline Monroe, whom I would come to know as my mother. Caroline would take me to her sister whenever she had to work a late night shift. Her sister's name is Carma." *Aunt C.* Understanding floods my mind as I realize why Mama C is so affectionate to him.

He continues, "At the time, it was just Mr. Washington, Aunt C, Jack and Kim. The adults saw my potential and pointed it out to Caroline and she in turn pointed it out to the system." He clears his throat. I look up to make sure he's okay. He glances at me and smiles.

"Before I knew it," he says. "I was getting shuttled into fully-funded acceleration programs." He gives me a wry smile. "I know what it's like to be tested non-stop."

I smile back in amusement.

"I guess it helped in the long run, though. I graduated from high school when I was twelve," he says casually. He says it like a weatherman would say it's sunny all week.

"*Twelve?*" I repeat. "You graduated from high school when you were *twelve?*"

He just nods like it's no big deal.

"Goddamn," I mutter to myself. Immediately, he winces.

"Please don't say that."

"Sorry," I reply. "I forgot you're religious."

He smiles and shakes his head. "Jesus is my savior not my religion. The crew at the shelter...my church...they're all the family I've ever known."

I nod in acceptance. I can understand that.

"When did you become a Christian?" I ask.

He looks at me in surprise.

He answers, "My mom was always a believer. So were the folks at the shelter. But I guess I didn't really start living it out until a couple of years ago…around the same time she passed away. Breast cancer."

"I'm so sorry."

"Me too. Imagine if she had just held on one more year…"

That sentence makes me pause. He's right. If we had known what my blood could do before she passed away, she would be safe and healthy as we speak. The magnitude of what my blood can do…what *I* can do for others is beginning to take shape in my mind.

"Jason? You know I want to help people, don't you?"

He frowns in confusion. "Of course you do."

"I don't know if this friend of yours will be able to isolate the protein or harvest the cure. But I want you to know that I *want* him to. Not just for my sake."

Jason nods. He gets it. I backtrack to his faith.

"Tell me more about Christianity."

"What do you want to know?"

"What does it mean to be a Christian? What do you believe?"

He lets out a low whistle. "That's a lot to deliver."

"Try." I like this. I like that we can talk about religion – even though we're not supposed to, even though it's not "PC."

"I became a Christian when I gave my life to Christ. Meaning, I accepted that Jesus died on the cross, rose again, and is the ultimate atonement for my sins. I accept him as my Savior and as a believer I try to model my life after him."

"So you believe he's the son of God?"

"Yes. And that he is God."

"Huh?"

"The incarnation. It's complicated. Have you heard of the trinity?"

I remember what Isaiah told me. "One God, three persons, three in one?"

"Yeah, that's what I believe."

"Do you believe in hell?" I ask.

He nods.

"How do you know where you're going?"

"Once I accepted Christ, I was destined for heaven."

He sounds so sure. So positive. For a few moments we're both quiet. I pick up the conversation on a different track this time.

"You've given up a lot for me," I begin.

He shakes his head.

"Enough about me," he says. "Tell me more about your life growing up. Who were your friends?"

I grow uncomfortable.

"I don't have any friends."

I let the admission hang dead in the air and stare at the rolling wheat fields that pass us outside.

"Why not?" he asks in a very serious tone.

I know he can tell I don't want to talk about this. But he pushes me anyway.

"Can I be honest with you?" he asks. "I noticed you in the hospital. The night of your brother's accident. I noticed that you weren't talking to anyone and they weren't talking to you."

"So you noticed that I was a weirdo –"

"Absolutely not," he says. "I noticed that the people around you were inconsiderate jerks who didn't have the decency to try and comfort you during such a difficult time."

I look at him and can see the flare of anger in his eyes and it bowls me over. Maybe I'm not crazy. Maybe my isolation isn't entirely my fault. I think about my mom's letter to me and recognize that she and Dad made a choice too. When I withdrew, they *chose* not to engage with me. They chose to let me be. And so did everyone else around me. Whether or not I withdrew from people, a relationship is a two-way street and it wasn't all on me.

"When I was little," I explain. "I was a painfully shy child. I found it difficult to hold conversations with my parents much less strangers. My parents took me to a psychiatrist at some point to see what was wrong and he diagnosed me with –"

"Social anxiety disorder?" he asks.

I smile. "Sometimes I forget you're a doctor."

"Can't turn it off. Sorry."

"Don't be. Anyway, he said I would grow out of it. When it came time for me to start school, the other kids noticed my quiet behavior and pegged me as someone to stay away from. So I got used to it and didn't reach out. I…I don't know what it means to have a friend. I only know what it looks like on screen."

He clears his throat and I think he's about to say something but he doesn't. I glance at him and can see that his eyes are more teary than usual.

"It's okay," I reassure him. "I'm used to it. People don't see me."

"That's not true," he says. "I see you."

CHAPTER TEN

Nicolette:

Between the bathroom breaks, gas breaks, and meal breaks, it takes us a total of twelve hours to travel from Seattle to Yreka, California; a town so green and so small, it's a wonder there are any people in this ridiculously rural area. The sun is starting to set and Jason has to put all of his attention into navigating the narrow, mountainous roads safely.

Tried and true, the GPS leads us directly to Eva Bond's compact, two story cabin. It looks like something out of an Aspen-based movie, minus the snow. As he drives up the driveway, a young, tall, thin, strikingly beautiful black woman walks out of the lit cabin. She's wearing all black: black jeans, black shirt, black leather jacket. Even black earrings. Her hair is arranged in a small, neat afro and her skin is a deep dark brown. She's absolutely stunning. Jason pops the locks and jumps out to meet her. I follow suit.

"Jason!" She gives him a quick hug. "Longtime no see."

She extends her hand to me. "You must be Nicolette. I'm Eva Bond."

"Nice to meet you, Eva. Thank you so much for having us."

"Sure thing. Let me help you with those."

The cabin is small but very beautiful. Plush beige carpets line most of the flooring in the house. In other parts, there are light, golden hardwood floors. It looks like something out of an HGTV show. We each have our own rooms. Once we're settled in, we eat a light dinner and Jason fills in the holes for Eva.

"What happened to your siblings?" she asks me.

"I don't know," I reply. "They ran the same time I did so my hope is that they're laying low. I have no idea how to reach them without endangering them."

She nods with a contemplative expression on her face.

"So," she turns to Jason. "You're harboring a fugitive of the law and asking me to do the same?"

Way to be blunt.

"Well, when you put it like that…" Jason is speechless.

"Don't worry, Jay-Jay. I'll help you. As soon as Isaiah mentioned you, I was in. I'll be happy to help your girlfriend."

Whoa! What?

Jason looks at me and back at her. "Umm, no it's not like that. We're just friends."

I try to get past that statement. He's right. We never made any sort of commitment to each other. We haven't even talked about the kiss that almost took place last night. The truth is we are just friends. But it doesn't sit well with me.

"'Just friends?'" she repeats. He nods but she just looks at him, a small smile playing on her lips. His expression slightly alters as he holds her stare.

I look between the two of them.

"What am I missing?" I ask.

She addresses me but raises her eyebrow at Jason. "He didn't tell you?"

"Not yet," he says. He takes a swig of his water—

"Well, now's as good a time as ever," she says with an amused smile. "I popped Jason's cherry back in the day."

—and coughs most of it up. I clap him on the back and Eva passes him a napkin.

"I don't get it. I thought you were a Christian." I ask him.

"This was before I accepted Christ," he explains in between coughs.

I look down at my plate. I don't know what to think. I have no right to be angry but I can still feel the tingling of jealousy rise in my chest. So they had a past. Not that I can blame either of them - she's stunningly gorgeous and so is he. In spite of my feelings, I can readily admit that they would make a ridiculously attractive couple - and a stunning set of babies.

Do they still have feelings for each other? I look up and find Eva watching me and I have my answer. Everything in her eyes and demeanor is telling me that she's over him. Helping him out for old time's sake. She smiles a secret smile to me and I know what she's trying to tell me. I smile back in appreciation. While Jason recovers from his coughing fit, I try to get to know her better.

"How do you and Jason know each other?" I ask.

"Harvest Hope. My mom was a frequent resident there so I kind of grew up with the crew. I stayed in touch."

"What do you do?"

She smiles another secretive smile. "Oh, this and that. Mostly government work. You'll find out soon enough."

How incredibly vague. Now I'm really intrigued.

"So, why did Isaiah have us stop here?"

She leans forward. "Is it true that you're heading to San Diego?" I nod. "Well, I guess he figured you could use some self-defense skills. I can teach you those and help you stock up for the journey."

"Stock up?"

"You'll see," she smiles.

She wasn't kidding. The next day, immediately after breakfast, Eva takes us to her attic. To my surprise, what I expect to be filled with moldy boxes and random knickknacks is instead filled with rifles, pistols, AK-47s and a slew of arsenal I've never seen in person. Silver case upon silver case are stacked around the perimeter of the room, holding God-only-knows what, along with a tiny refrigerator and freezer unit. There's a large padded surface in the middle of the floor space and a boxing bag, hanging at the corner of it. Eva walks to the far side of the room, turning on one of the four computers lined across the counter.

Jason takes one look at my face and explains.

"Eva is a freelance assassin," he whispers. "She works almost exclusively for the government."

"'Almost?'" I ask.

"Yeah," she says from across the room. "It's nice to make a little extra cash on the side."

Her hearing is amazing.

"What about Isaiah?" I ask. "Why does he know so much about search dogs and hiding places?"

"He used to work with the CIA." Jason answers.

I'm still trying to digest this information when Eva walks up to us and holds out a pair of sleeveless grip gloves in one hand, an alcohol swab, syringe and needle in the other.

"Before we begin, I would be remiss if I were to say I'm helping you simply out of the goodness of my heart."

I give her a questioning look.

"Blood. I need a sample of your blood for future insurance." I look at Jason and he nods. I hold out my arm and Jason draws the blood. He hands the syringe back to Eva.

"Thank you." She takes it, pulls the needle, seals the syringe, labels it and stores it in the freezer.

"Alright," she turns back to us. "Let's begin."

Within minutes she has us doing drills. She starts off slow with jumping jacks, push-ups, and running in place. Then she gets intense: suicide drills, core workouts, and punching rounds. Sweat pours off of me and Jason is only doing slightly better.

"Okay, warm up's over," she says.

"Warm up?!" I pant.

She starts with basic self-defense skills, knee to the groin moves and such. But her lesson quickly becomes more complex. She teaches us how to disarm an opponent. What mindset to have when facing an enemy.

"They're no longer human," she says. "They're target points. A collection of organs just waiting for you to destroy." She touches the center of my chest. "Sternum. Drive your elbow into it with the weight of your body, you can snap it in pieces." Her hands move down. "Liver. One area not covered by the ribs. Great target for incapacitation." They move back up to my face. "Eyes. Gouge them out. A blind enemy is an ineffective one. Ears. Clap them hard and cause auditory confusion. Nose. Hit with the heel of your palm and break it. Neck. Strike hard enough and you'll knock them unconscious. Bones. Snap them like you would a piece of wood. Whatever you do, Nicolette," she says. "Go for the kill."

She makes us practice on each other. Each target of the body over and over and over again. When she thinks we've mastered it, she steps in and has us practice with her. She takes no prisoners. Each time we try to restrain her, she manages to get a hold of us.

"The people who are after you are just as skilled if not more skilled than myself," she warns. "You *have* to beat me. Otherwise you have no chance of beating them."

We try again. And again. And again. And again. Hours pass and we still can't beat her.

But we do improve.

Finally a breakthrough hits when she and I combat. I manage to block all of her blows and swipe her under the legs. I demonstrate how I would further incapacitate her if she were a real enemy and she gives me the green light. She and Jason go a couple more rounds before she gives him the green light as well. By the time she approves both of us, it feels like second nature. I know what to do with my body and what it is capable of doing. I know which parts to protect the most.

It's dark out when she calls it a day. We quickly eat and head to bed, a full day waiting for us tomorrow. Jason stretches his shoulders as we walk down the hall to my room.

"I've never been so sore in my life."

"Are you sure about that?" I tease. He rolls his eyes. I walk ahead of him to reach my room but he pulls me back.

"Are you okay?" he asks.

"I'm fine. Why?"

"No, I mean about Eva. About… our past."

"Oh. Yeah, I'm fine." I frown. "Why wouldn't I be?"

He shrugs. "I don't know."

"It's not like we have anything going on."

I can't believe I just said that. His eyebrows shoot up in surprise and he looks down at his feet.

"Yeah," he says. "I guess you're right."

Great. I'm painfully aware of the fact that this could have been our chance to clear the air. My chance to tell him how I feel. But I just blew it. And I don't know how to get it back. He meets my eyes and smiles down at me. I smile back but on the inside, I feel like crying.

"Good night, Nicolette."

"Good night, Jason."

Jason:

The next day is all guns. Marksmanship, targets, loading, classification, disarming and re-arming. Eva sticks with three "basic" weapons: a Glock 26 pistol, AK-47, and M16 rifles. She teaches us how to load and unload each weapon, when to use which one, and how to handle them. We practice shooting targets on her vast backyard and I notice that she doesn't have any neighboring homes. She stands beside a very large black tote and pulls out equipment after equipment.

"The Glock 26 is your carry-on. Use this when you have to conceal your weapons. The AK-47s and M16s are fully rigged to operate full auto."

"Wait." I ask, "Isn't that illegal?"

"For you it is. Not for me. Technically, I'm not even supposed to have these guns in this state but I have clearance."

"But we don't," I point out. "What if we get stopped and are found with –"

"That's what these are for." She hands Nicolette and me a pair of documents. False authorization and registration for all three of the weapons. Nicolette looks at her agape.

"How did you do this?"

"I called a favor," she replies. I know that's all the explanation we're going to get from her.

"Thank you, Eva."

"Don't thank me yet." She pulls out two silver cell phones from the bag. "Prepaid, untraceable phones. I'll trade you."

We hand her our cell phones and she takes a hammer, smashing them to pieces in the grass. She turns back to us. She holds out a tiny silver device. It's shaped like the half of a cashew. She hands it to Nicolette.

"Recording device," she says. "Virtually undetectable. Put it in a place with enough heat and it will turn on automatically – ten hours of memory."

She leans close to Nic and whispers something in her ear.

I give them a questioning look.

"We didn't want to make you uncomfortable," Eva quips. She turns back to Nic, "I called another favor on your behalf."

"What do you mean?" Nic asks.

Eva hands her a slip of paper. "Your siblings are in France. Apparently President François Hollande has agreed to grant them exile in Bordeaux but the news hasn't broken out yet. They purchased a flat there under an alias. I wrote their number down for you."

Nicolette stares at the paper for several long minutes. Eva looks at me in concern. I shrug. Finally, Nic folds the paper, places it into her jeans and gives Eva a long, thankful hug.

When she pulls back, we can both see that she's crying.

Eva looks uncomfortable. "I just wanted to help. It's no big deal." She looks at me. "I'll let you take care of the tears and…stuff." She walks back into the cabin.

I nod and take her place, folding Nic in my arms.

After a few minutes, she calms down and steps back with, "I need to call them."

I nod and let her go off to make the call. Now that we're both armed with untraceable phones, this is the perfect time for me to make my own.

"Hello?"

"Greg, it's me."

"Jason!" his relieved voice fills my ears. "Jason, thank God you're alright. Where are you?"

"I'm in California."

"California! What the hell are you doing over there?"

"We're getting help. It's a long story."

"Is she alright?" he asks.

"Yeah, she's fine. Less shaky."

"Good. Good. So…what are your plans?"

"I have a friend I'm planning to see but before we get there, I'm thinking of giving Nic a surprise. Can you keep a secret?"

Nicolette:

I never thought I would be so happy to hear my sister's voice. I caught the two of them right before they were headed to bed, nine hours ahead of us, five thousand miles away.

"Nikki, how on earth did you find us?" Natalia asks. "No one knows we're here yet."

"A friend of a friend of a friend who's connected to high places," I reply. "How on earth did you get there?"

"Jack Hafer – Dad's attorney. He helped us charter a private plane and we went straight to the French consulate for help."

"Why France?"

"It's the only place where I speak the language fluently. And President Hollande was willing to grant us political asylum so we jumped on it."

I can hear Nate in the background, "Where is she? Is she okay?"

"I'm fine," I answer. "Jason's helping me."

"So the media *did* get something right."

"You heard what Carter said about Mom and Dad?"

"Yes. The little bitch. There was no 'self-defense.' Mom and Dad were trying to defend themselves *and* us. At least they buried them."

"How do you know that?"

"Hollande met with us briefly and gave us the scoop."

They update me on how they're settling in Bordeaux. Nate's already enrolled at the local school and Natalia is finishing her degree at *Université Michel de Montaigne Bordeaux Trois*. I talk to Nate briefly and promise to call them when I'm more settled.

I walk across the lawn and meet Jason midway as he tucks his cell phone in his pocket.

"How are they?" he asks.

"They're good." I relay the conversation to him as we walk back to the cabin.

"And they're sure they can trust Hollande?" Jason asks.

"Yeah. He hasn't caused them any concern or alarm yet." I switch topics, "So who exactly are we trying to meet in San Diego?"

"Nicholas Rincon. He's a hematology specialist in his area. I interned with him prior to my residency. The sooner we get to him, the better."

Brooklyn:

"What's the latest?" I ask.

I pace the office, too anxious to stay put. Kennedy and Agent Dannican sit before me. Agent Dannican, a tall bald man in his late thirties glances at Kennedy. I already know what he's going to say.

"Madame President, Miss Talloway and her accomplice are still missing. Our teams have scoured the state of Washington and have yet to find them."

"For God's sake," I snap. "This is an eighteen-year-old kid. How far can she go?"

Kennedy winces at my tone. He glances at Dannican before turning to me.

"Madame President, Agent Dannican would like to expand the search to a national level."

"Why?"

Dannican speaks up, "There is a very high possibility that she is no longer in Washington State."

"I thought you secured the border, *Agent* Dannican," I say, one brow raised in irritation.

"We did, Madame. To the best of our ability but there is no guarantee that every single toll person, ship captain, or even airline personnel remained vigilant the entire time."

This is the last thing I need to hear. If he's right and she did manage to leave the state, then we have as much of a chance of finding her as we do finding a needle in a haystack. A White House Aid knocks on the door and enters.

"Excuse me, Madame President," she says. "But I have President Slovachi on line four. He says it's urgent."

That's what they all say. It's "urgent" – like no one else on this planet has sick, dying citizens to take care of. I voice none of this, of course. I simply nod.

"Thank you."

She's not done. "President Titsu and Ambassador Han are still holding."

I sigh, "Okay."

She looks at Kennedy, "We also need your statement regarding the search and –"

"Okay!" I snap. "Enough!"

She turns a deep shade of crimson and Kennedy gestures for her to leave. She nods politely and quietly closes the door. I walk to my desk and am greeted by piles of papers: memos, faxes, letters – all strewn across my desk. I try to rub the stress out of my eyes and look back up to find both men watching me.

"President Hollande has granted Natalia and Nathaniel Talloway political asylum. I received the notice from him personally this morning."

The men look at each other in shock. Kennedy looks dumbfounded but Agent Dannican has a thoughtful frown.

"At least we know where they are," he says.

"Excuse me?" I ask. "This is not good news. Do you realize how this makes me look? How this makes my country look?" my voice rises. "That two kids would rather seek exile in *France* than stay in their own country!"

"I don't get it," Kennedy shakes his head. "Why would Hollande agree to this?"

"Why wouldn't he?" I answer. "If France is friendly to her siblings, there's a greater chance the girl will be friendly to them. She might even *join* them in exile."

"We can't let that happen."

"Exactly," I reply. I look at Agent Dannican. "*You* can't let that happen. Expand your search and for God's sake find her!"

CHAPTER ELEVEN

Jason:

Once again, we leave early in the morning, while it's still dark. The drive takes about ten hours and we make a few pit stops on the way. I stop in Santa Clarita and rest for a good hour. She makes no objections and raises no questions.

When we reach Anaheim, I watch her out of the corner of my eye. She looks around in curiosity which quickly turns into confusion when I enter the Disneyland parking lot and pay for a space. I park the car, take note of its location and pull out some water bottles. She watches me the whole time waiting for an explanation. I look up at her and say one word.

"Surprise."

"No way," she says. I nod. "No way!"

I explain, "You've been so stressed this entire trip. This is on the way to San Diego so I figured why not stop and have some fun?"

"Are you sure you're not too tired?"

"I'm fine. That nap in Santa Clarita cleared my head."

She smiles in understanding. "So that's what that was for."

She pauses in thought and frowns.

"Jason, are you sure?"

I know what she's asking and I'm prepared for that too. I pull out a pair of colored contact lenses and hand them to her.

"I got it at one of the stops," I explain. "They're looking for a chick with long black hair and stunning hazel eyes." She rolls them at me for good measure. "I'm sitting next to a girl with short blonde hair and soon-to-be blue eyes."

It takes her a few minutes but she manages to pop the contact lenses in her eyes and turns to me with a mischievous expression.

"How do I look?"

"Incredible." She takes my breath away.

She smiles and asks, "But what about you?"

I pull out my baseball cap and place the rim close to my eyes. She smiles and leans in close to me. She throws her arms around me and pulls me into a hug that catches me by surprise.

"Thank you," she whispers.

I hesitate…and then pull her close. Holding her feels so perfect. After a few moments we pull back and look at each other for a long moment. I can feel the heat rising in my blood and I know we need to get out of this car.

"Jason –"

I put my index finger against her lips. She touches my hand and I move it to her cheek. She turns into it and kisses my palm.

"Don't mention it," I reply.

Nicolette:

I can't believe he's done this for me. No one has ever taken the time to surprise me. The last time I went to Disneyland, I was like seven and I hardly remember anything about the trip except that it was one of the few times in my life when I didn't feel invisible. There's something about traveling that makes parents extra attentive about keeping track of their children.

But I'm not a kid anymore. I can remember everything about this trip. And I'm with someone who has intentionally planned this and cares about me. *"I see you,"* he said. I don't know what Jason and I are. Do friends interact the way he and I interact? Do friends give up everything - home, career and other friends - to protect a friend? Do friends almost kiss each other?

Jason pays for our tickets in cash and we make it through the shoddy security relatively easy. For safety measures, he disassembled the Glock

26 and hid it within the layers of our sweatshirts. He also packed a first aid kit that the security guard frowned at but eventually shrugged off.

The weather is perfect for amusement park walking and even though it's summer and the park is still crowded, we have a good time getting to know each other even in the ridiculously long lines. Everything is paid for in cash – food, memorabilia, and souvenirs. We trek through Fantasyland briefly before moving on to Frontierland and Adventureland – the most laid-back parts of the park. In Frontierland, we spend close to an hour scoping out the pins in the Westward Ho shop, making small talk with the very friendly "cast members". My people-watching is on overdrive as I observe family after family, couple after couple interacting with each other and trying to have a good time. Most of the couples are enjoying the park effortlessly. Most of the pint sized children I see are enjoying the day, some girls occasionally passing in their Cinderella, Belle, and Princess Tiana costumes. Then there are the kids who aren't having the best day; some are so small, they haven't the slightest compunction about throwing a red-faced, tear streaming, eardrum-bursting temper tantrum in front of complete strangers. One look at the parents' faces makes me seriously second-guess ever reproducing myself.

In the "New Orleans" part of the park we come across an old caricature artist named Henry and ask him to draw the two of us. It only takes a few minutes and he holds out the final picture to us.

"Whoa!" Jason says. "I didn't know my mouth was that big."

"I did," I reply.

"Hey!"

"Kidding," I giggle. "Just kidding! Thank you so much, Henry."

The old man with glittering green eyes smiles.

"You're very welcome, young lady." He looks between the two of us. "How long have you two been going steady?"

"'Going steady?'"

"Dating."

I look at Jason, completely caught off guard.

I stammer, "Oh no, we're not –"

"We're just friends," Jason says beside me.

The man doesn't look like he believes us. He has the same expression Eva had two days ago, another person - this one a complete stranger - who thinks we are together.

This is awkward and I really want to change the topic.

"Henry?" I ask. "I don't know if this is against the rules but would it be possible for me to draw you?"

His gray eyebrows shoot up in surprise.

"Miss, in all my thirty years as a caricature artist, I've never had a guest ask me that."

"So can she?" Jason asks.

"I don't see why not," he replies.

It takes me about double the time it took Henry to draw us but with his tips and advice, I manage to draw my very first caricature. Henry and Jason applaud me and I feel heat rise to my face. Henry asks to keep it so I initial the corner and hand it over to him.

"You are a fine artist, young lady. Do you plan on studying art?"

"I don't know," I reply. "I would like to-"

"Good! You should! Learn and make the most of your craft while you can. In a few years, I won't be able to do this anymore."

"What do you mean?" I ask.

"I have Parkinson's," he says matter-of-factly. "I'm in the early stages of it but I know my drawing days are coming to a close."

It's amazing how a complete stranger can come to mean a great deal to you in the span of only half an hour. I think of Henry five or even two years down the line with shaky hands. Unable to hold a toothbrush steady much less do what he loves for a living. Henry busies himself with cleaning his tools and I pull Jason aside.

"I want to help him," I say urgently.

"With what?"

"His Parkinson's."

He initially frowns in confusion before understanding dawns on him. His eyes widen and he shakes his head vehemently.

"Are you nuts?"

"Maybe, but that's beside the point."

"Nicolette, do you know how many things can go wrong? What if he outs us?" he whispers, glancing at Henry.

"He won't."

I know he won't.

"Jason, please. I have to help him."

Jason runs his hand through his hair and sighs.

"Okay."

Jason:

The first aid kit came in handy. I almost wish I left it in the car. Nicolette, Henry and I are all crowded into the handicap stall of the men's bathroom in Adventureland. Henry sits on the toilet with the sleeve of his left arm pulled up. I dig into the backpack and pull out the kit stocked with gauze, bandages, alcohol swabs, a hypodermic needle and syringe.

I clean the needle with alcohol; sterilize Henry and Nicolette's arms. The procedure is pretty simple: I draw blood from Nicolette first and then insert her blood into one of Henry's veins before wrapping both arms with gauze.

"Okay," I whisper. "We're done."

I look at Nic.

"You should leave first." I hand her my baseball cap and jacket. "Be careful."

"I will," she whispers. "Thank you, Jason."

She turns to Henry, shakes his hand and says goodbye. He holds her a second longer and whispers, "Thank you *so* much, dear."

She smiles and ducks out. When I turn back, I find Henry watching me. He extends his hand to me and promises yet again that he won't say a word.

"Take care of her, son" he says solemnly.

I nod and exit next.

Nicolette:

Jason and I walk side-by-side down Main Street. I've given him his jacket and baseball cap back. We look ahead and keep quiet for the first few minutes as we walk in step.

"Thank you," I repeat.

"It was your decision."

"I know but it was a huge risk."

"Why did you do it?"

I shrug. "He needed help. I could help him."

"You could help others."

I look at him sharply. "What are you trying to say?"

"Nothing…just that," he pauses. "You could help millions – billions – of people the same way you just helped Henry."

Doesn't he get it?

"I was never against helping people. I was against giving up my life to do it."

He remains quiet.

I continue, "I just wish I didn't have this. I wish this didn't exist, you know?"

He shakes his head. "No, I don't know. Nic, you have a gift, a God-given gift. You can do something in one minute that I've spent nearly ten years studying to do."

Now I'm quiet. He pulls me over to an empty bench in front of one of the fake homes on Main Street and lowers his voice.

"Did you ever stop to think that maybe you have this blood for a reason?" he asks.

I bristle. "That reason got my parents killed."

He looks down at his feet.

"In some ways," I continue. "It must be nice never having known your parents. You can imagine them however you want…that they loved you. Adored you."

He shakes his head irritably. "I can hardly imagine having loving parents when they abandoned me at the hospital."

I wince. What was I thinking?

"Jason, I'm sorry. What I meant was-"

"Besides," he cuts me off. "I'd take eighteen years with them over any imagination. Your parents loved you, Nicolette. They stood by you. They *died* for you."

The words rock me for a moment. How can a fact so painful be so comforting at the same time?

"I think that's the hardest part," I admit, tears welling in my eyes. "Knowing they loved me after they died but never knowing it when they were alive."

He pulls me to him and holds me for a few minutes. No words to fill the space, just arms to make me feel safe. I shake off the wave of emotion and we agree to do some more souvenir shopping before taking off. We hang out at the Emporium for a half hour. I hand Jason my bottle and sweater.

"I'm gonna use the restroom."

As I sit in the stall, I look down at my feet. I hear someone open the stall to my left and hear the sound of combat boots. My gaze shifts to the left and I see a pair of feet in what has to be at least four-inch thick heels. Who in their right mind wears *combat boots* to an amusement park? I look to my right and as I expected, all the feet I see are adorned in sneakers, flip-flops or flats. Even stranger is the fact that the boots are tucked with black cargo pants – not jeans, no shorts, but black pants in the middle of a summer day. I get up, flush my toilet, and head over to the sinks. The woman on my left leaves her stall at the exact same time.

I can feel the hairs standing on the back of my neck. Something isn't right and I can't shake the feeling away. The woman is a tall, brunette with an athletic build, dressed in the pants, boots, and a thin sweater. I wash my hands and she washes hers next to me, on my left. I look over and notice that they are lined with rings. I look up and catch her staring at me in the reflection of the mirror. She quickly looks away when I catch her eyes. I turn off the tap and turn to grab a paper towel. In the reflection of the mirrors, I catch her in motion.

She lunges at me with her fist. I turn, block the blow, and deliver one of my own. The woman falls back with a gasp of surprise but quickly rebounds.

I go into tunnel mode. I can barely hear the women and children screaming around us. Out of my peripheral vision, I see them running to the exit in horror.

She quickly recovers - bounces back up and goes for another blow, one that I duck. I grab the arm she's extended and snap it against my foot like a twig. She screams in pain and clutches her mangled limb. I grab her shoulders and drive my knee into the center of her chest. She grunts in pain and falls down to the floor. I run for the exit but she catches my foot with her other arm and trips me. My head explodes in pain as my forehead makes contact with the hard, tiled ground.

I turn on my back and just miss the edge of her combat boot heel crashing down on the ground next to my ear.

"I need backup," the woman says. At first I think she's talking to me but then I realize she must be talking into a radio feed or something.

"No, we've been staked here all day. I'm not letting her go!"

She pounces on me and uses her working fist to hit me across the cheek. With the rings she's wearing, it feels like I've been hit by a block of steel. She starts to choke me in a vice grip with the same hand. Even though she's partially incapacitated, she's really strong. I'm starting to lose oxygen, my vision is swimming.

I grab her neck and pull her close to me with the crook of my left arm. I use my other hand to hook the curve of my thumb into her left eye. I dig deep, hard, and fast and feel the juice of her eye socket squirt into my face. She reels back and screams in agony, letting me loose. Across the floor, a small orb, her eye ball, bounces over to the nearest toilet. The woman rocks back and forth as she clings to her empty eye socket, blood streaming past her hand, screaming all the while.

I run over to the bathroom exit but stop mid-run. Several security guards are racing over towards us. I backpedal, run past the woman, now curled in a ball, and enter the handicap stall. There's a window right above it. I climb onto the toilet, use the tampon trash as leverage, and pull myself through the window. Behind me I hear several feet run in.

"Stop right there!"

They're too late. I jump through the window and land on my knees. I feel a pair of hands pick me up. I pivot to plant a blow but Jason blocks it.

"Come on!"

We're lucky. Everyone is gathered around the front of the restroom exit. Jason hands me his baseball cap and jacket once again. We power walk out of the park as more and more people crowd around that bathroom.

CHAPTER TWELVE

Jason:

We walk out of the park to keep from alerting the authorities or anyone else around us. Try to act natural in front of the staff as we make our way to the shuttle and then to the car. I fight every urge to hightail it out of the parking lot. As soon as we're free of the park, Anaheim, and back on the freeway, we talk.

"How did this happen?" Nic asks.

"I don't know."

We were careful. We were so careful. Nic tells me everything that happened in that bathroom. I explain that I went to the back of the restroom when I overheard people reporting a fight.

"It wasn't Henry," she says adamantly. "It couldn't have been. She said they had been staked there all day."

My blood runs cold.

She looks at me. "What?"

"I know who it was."

She looks at me in surprise. "Who?"

"There's only one person who knew where we were going before we got there."

Brooklyn:

I pace in the office again.

"What's next on their agenda?" I ask him.

Greg McGrath shrugs, "He didn't tell me."

"You can't be serious," Kennedy snaps.

"Yes, I am serious. Had I known you were going to screw up so royally, believe me, I would have asked more questions."

"I wasn't on the field, McGrath. Dannican was."

"Why don't you fire that idiot?" McGrath replies. "He didn't take my tip seriously and sent in some rookie idiot who was dumb enough to wear boots on the job. Pretty conspicuous if you ask me."

"Dannican is the best in this field –"

"Doesn't look like it."

"Better question: why didn't you let Dannican apprehend him at the hospital when he had the chance?"

"Jason wouldn't tell *me* where she was, even when he trusted me. I needed to keep up the appearance of loyalty until we could get him and the girl together."

"How brilliant of you," Kennedy replies snidely.

"Better than what you've contributed."

"Enough!" I shout. Both men shut up. "What's done is done. So stop arguing and think. Where could they be headed next?"

McGrath frowns and shakes his head. "I gave him the name of a friend but I doubt he'll be going there now."

"What about the AMA?" Kennedy suggests.

"No, too obvious. What about surveillance cameras on the lots?"

I shake my head. "Do you know how many vehicles enter, park and leave Disneyland per hour?"

"They're on the run and they have to improvise. Who would Jason turn to besides me?" McGrath thinks for a moment. "Yes. *Yes!*"

We look at him in inquiry. McGrath ignores Kennedy and looks at me.

"Call your men. Get better ones this time. I just got you another lead."

Nicolette:

We head straight to San Diego and make no pit stops on the way. I glance at Jason's stoic profile in the dark. I can tell he's still shaken up over Dr. McGrath's betrayal. From what he's told me about their relationship, Jason looked up to him as a friend, a mentor, and even a father-figure. I don't know what to say to try and comfort him. I'm still trying to collect myself after what happened in the park. We barely got out by the skin of our teeth. My cheek is throbbing and I can tell it's beginning to swell.

I turn on the radio in the hopes of drowning out my thoughts with music. Big mistake. The announcer gives a newsreel and of course we're in it:

"There was a reported sighting of Nicolette Talloway, the teenager whose blood has curative properties. Authorities report that she was sighted at the Disneyland Resort in Anaheim, California after engaging in a confrontation with a federal agent in one of the restrooms. It is unclear if the 18-year-old was accompanied by suspected accomplice, Dr. Jason Monroe. Authorities state that Talloway changed her appearance. She now reportedly has short blonde hair –"

Jason turns off the radio and quickly changes lanes. He gets off the next exit and goes straight to a gas station. He wordlessly pulls on his baseball cap, enters the store and makes a purchase. I wait in the car, slouching in my seat to reduce passerby visibility. I pull out the cashew shaped device from my pocket and toy with it. Why would Eva give me this?

He emerges a few moments later with what looks like a box of hair dye. He gets in, hands it to me and gets back on the freeway. "Radiant Amber" the box reads.

"Why don't I ever get to choose?"

"Sorry," he smiles. "Next time I'll ask."

"What you said earlier –"

"I don't want to talk about McGrath."

"No, at the park...the whole God...thing."

He glances at me.

"Assuming that he exists –"

"He does exist."

"How do you know?"

"How do you think you came to exist? How do you think the Earth, the sun and the moon came to exist? Do you really believe that Big Bang theory? That everything in its intricate design and function came out of thin air from no Creator at all?"

I don't. The conclusion comes to me swiftly and I'm able to accept it.

"What could God want me to do with this blood?"

"I don't know, Nic." he says quietly. "But at the end of the day, it's up to you to do it. Whatever it is."

Great.

Brooklyn:

I walk down the hall of this historic home and think of all the men who walked this hall before me. They too heard the clicks of cameras, the murmurs of reporters, the busy feet of staff. They too felt the eyes of an entire nation watching in rapt attention. Now it is my turn...to address the nation.

The teleprompter roles before me and I begin just as rehearsed:

"My fellow Americans. This afternoon at approximately 6:29PM Pacific Standard Time, Nicolette Talloway was spotted at the Disneyland Resort in Anaheim, California. An incident ensued between Miss Talloway and a federal agent and the agent in question was severely injured as a result of the altercation." I pause for effect. "I want to make it known that my administration is not pursuing Miss Talloway in any sort of 'manhunt.' We simply want to speak to Miss Talloway about exploring the possibility of helping others with her unique ability - the ability to cure previously incurable diseases."

As I speak, Dannican's men are loading their weapons, reviewing their artillery and strategizing over the next sting. I ignore the reality of my lie and continue:

"I want to make it clear that I do not want a single hair on Miss Talloway's head harmed. Regardless of what her blood can do, she is still an American citizen. This is her home. We are her people. We do care." I look more intently into the camera.

"Nicolette, if you are watching this, I urge you to accept the help that we are offering. We wish you no harm. We want to help you and protect you. There are many people internationally who seek your blood. Trust in us, and we will keep you safe." I straighten and assume a somber expression. "May God bless you, your family and these great United States of America."

I turn and walk down the hall. As soon as I turn the corner into another hall, away from the cameras, Kennedy meets me.

"Are they set?" I ask.

"Affirmative."

Jason:

The drive to Nicholas Rincon's place takes two hours. He lives in a nice, relatively quiet neighborhood. We pull up to his driveway and walk down the manicured pathway to his door.

Nicholas is a tall, athletic man in his late thirties with short blonde hair he tends to crop in a buzz cut. When he opens the door, his mouth drops in astonishment.

"Jason!" It takes a fraction of a second for his eyes to land on Nic and when they do, they grow even wider. He looks around and urges us to get in quickly. Closing the door, he turns to me and shakes his head in wonder.

"So it is true. How the hell did you get out of there?"

"Don't ask," I reply. I turn to Nic. "Nicolette Talloway, meet Dr. Nicholas Rincon, the nation's most underrated and brilliant hematologists. Nicholas, meet Nicolette."

They shake hands as Nicholas says, "Nice to meet you. You can call me Nick."

"Same here...but Nikki," she smiles. He smiles back in understanding.

Nicolette:

Nicholas takes us to his living room…or what's left of it. Books and papers are strewn across the room. A small sofa is pushed to one side of the room and a makeshift home lab is erected in the center of the living room, complete with translucent walls, a lab desk, patient bed, and computer.

"Holy crap," I murmur.

"Pretty cool, huh?" Nick says in a proud voice. "Jason just wishes he had this lab."

"Whatever makes you feel good," Jason replies.

"So I take it you're not married?" I ask.

Nick laughs. "Clearly I'm not. No woman in her right mind would live in this pigsty."

We all convene to the messy dining room and give Nick the basic details of our journey.

"Let me get this straight," Nick clarifies. "You want me to test Nikki's blood to see if we can isolate the protein that causes the cure? Haven't you guys already tried to?"

"Of course," Jason replies. "But so far we've had no success. I tried to add you to the case during the trials but Norris and McGrath wouldn't listen."

"Sorry we didn't call you ahead of time," he adds. "We were so focused on getting here untraced that we didn't stop to."

Nick shrugs, "It's fine. It's not like I have actual patients waiting for me tomorrow." He leans back in his seat. "So McGrath finally screwed you over, huh? I'm telling you, man, something was always shady about him. It's why I left."

Jason frowns. "You could have warned me."

"I did! You just didn't want to listen. As far as you were concerned, the sun *and* the moon shined out of his ass." He looks at me and smiles apologetically. "Excuse me."

"Oh, no worries."

Jason yawns and goes over to the kitchen adjoining the dining room. There are two refrigerators sitting there, both black. Jason opens one and finds several Petri dishes stacked on top of each other. He quickly closes it, opens the other fridge and digs in for food.

"Yeah, man, just help yourself," Nick quips sardonically.

He turns back to me and offers a gentle smile.

"Why don't you grab a bite to eat as well? Try to do it quickly and refrain from eating anything else between now and tomorrow morning. We'll test your blood then."

After I eat, I bid them both good night and head up to the guest room Nick directs me to. I take a shower and dye my hair with the kit Jason bought earlier. When I step out of the bathroom, I'm about to head to my room when I hear voices downstairs. Jason and Nicholas: they're still talking. I hear my name and perch myself at the top of the staircase, their voices carrying up their conversation to me like a carrier pigeon bringing me a letter.

"You are the last medical friend I can trust," Jason sighs.

"You know I won't tell anyone."

"Thanks."

"I like her," Nick says. "But, Jase, do you realize how much trouble you're in right now?"

"I know. I don't care. I have to help her. If it wasn't for me, she wouldn't be in this situation."

"That's not true," he points out. "They would have tested her blood regardless of your involvement. They test every family member when emergencies like this happen."

"I know, but I could have just lied and said her blood type didn't match...I could have done more to protect her during the clinicals, during the press release-"

"Bullshit. Hindsight is always twenty-twenty but we both know you're not helping her out of some contrived sense of duty. I'm not blind. I see the way you look at each other. There's something going on between the two of you."

I hold my breath and listen as hard as I can.

Jason sighs. "Nothing's happened between the two of us."

"Not yet, you mean."

"Not ever," Jason says with finality. "She deserves to have someone who is there for her without some ulterior motive."

"Jason, you can't help it if you like the girl."

"I don't just like her."

What? What does that mean?

He continues before Nick can probe. "I'm not leaving her, Nick - whatever that means for my future."

"Jason, this could end really badly."

"I know. But it won't end with her alone."

The next day Nicholas is in complete command. He tests my blood on several machines in the middle of his living room. Blood flows out of both of my arms and I keep my eyes fixed on the ceiling to take my mind off of it. Jason tries to help me relax, whispering reassuring words in my ear and rubbing my hands; but he also has to help Nick run the tests and analyze the data.

They look at data sheet after data sheet, pulling up different protein models on his computer, analyzing them. They keep talking about blood counts and cells, plasma and pH levels. They might as well be speaking in Dutch – I have no idea what the hell they're talking about. The analysis takes much longer than the actual blood test. I try to ignore them and read a book. My escape mechanism of choice isn't working so I dig out a sheet of paper and pencil and sketch the two of them, huddled together around the computer.

They're so absorbed in their work that by the time they notice me drawing them, I've almost completed the sketch. Several hours and two meals later, they pull back from their work.

"Okay," Nick announces. "We're done."

We gather around the dining table and eat dinner while Nick tries to relay their research to me in layman terms.

"You already know the basics of what your blood can do."

I nod.

"I tried to learn more about the extra protein in your blood that is essentially the cure." He looks at Jason and Jason nods. "Nicolette, the protein you produce is relatively combative by nature."

I frown. "What does that mean?"

Jason says, "It means that the protein will not allow itself to be detached from the other components of your blood. It literally clings to the other proteins and cells it came with like crazy glue on crack."

I know what they're trying to tell me so I just say it.

"The cure can't be isolated."

"No," Nick admits.

"And my blood can't be replicated."

"There isn't even a market for the replication of normal blood right now – much less blood like yours."

I bury my fingers in my hair. Words can't describe how disappointed I am. Jason and I came all this way with hope of the protein being isolated…only to find out what we already thought to be true. After all we've been through – it was all for nothing. We came all this way for nothing. And I'm pissed.

"What do we do now?" I amend myself, "What do *I* do now? Turn myself in?"

"No!" Jason replies. "We'll figure this out."

His words are comforting but it still doesn't answer the question of what to do. And if anything has become clear to me at this point, it's that the cards are in my hands. I have to decide what to do. I think about what Jason said earlier. There has to be a reason I have this blood. What am I supposed to do with it?

CHAPTER THIRTEEN

Nicolette:

We decide to leave the same night. Jason figures we can take a page from Natalia's book and charter a flight out of Mexico and make our next move there. It should only take us an hour to reach the border and once there, we figure we can bribe the authorities to let us through. We quickly re-pack our things and bid Nicholas farewell. He gives us some food for the trip and other supplies.

I buckle my seat belt as Jason starts the engine. I can't help but think this might be it. There might finally be a conclusion to this never-ending saga of running and hiding. I look out of the wing mirror on my side. It looks like a gaping black abyss outside. The night is so ink black nothing can be made out. Jason turns on the headlights and presses the brakes when suddenly I see a figure illuminated red.

Jason gasps beside me. He sees him too. There's more than one – as quick as they appear, several men surround the car in dark black uniforms.

"FREEZE!" *That voice.* "FBI!"

I know that voice.

"Mr. Talloway, I am under strict orders –"

"Get off of my property now!"

"Mr. Talloway –"

"You can't have her! What part of that don't you understand?"

"Sir, I am warning you to step aside!"

Jason reaches in the glove compartment for the gun.

"We can still get away."

"No!" I scream. I knock his hand out of the way. "They'll kill you."

"Fine." He pulls back, changes gears and backs the car out of the driveway. The men behind us jump out of the way, roll onto their backs and start to shoot as Jason changes gears. The rear windows shatter.

"Put your head down!" Jason yells.

I ignore him. I grab the gun, break the passenger window and fire back at the agents. It's no use though – they are impossible to see in the thick darkness. But apparently they can see me...

"Don't hit her!" I hear the head agent order.

I can smell the tires peel off the ground as Jason floors it. The agents continue to shoot, this time lower than before. We don't even make it to the next street before they blow out the two back tires. I duck back into the car and feel everything spin as the car reels out of control. Jason struggles to keep it from careening into a neighboring house. By the time the car is still, the agents bum rush the vehicle, weapons pointed.

"Unlock the doors now!" the agent orders.

"Nic, don't."

"Wait," I say.

I unclasp my seat belt, reach into my pocket and pull the cashew shaped device out. I reach into my shirt, past my bra and place it under my left breast. Jason looks at me quizzically.

"Just in case," I whisper. I pop the locks before he can protest. They pull me out of the car with rough hands and brace me against the vehicle. Several homes are lit, doors open with bewildered families looking out at the spectacle on the street. They cuff my hands. Jason catches my eye as he too gets cuffed.

"I'll get you out of this," he says.

I smile at him. We both know I'm in shit far too deep for any one person to pull me out. They whip me around as Nicholas runs up to the men, a shocked look on his face. He turns to Jason.

"Jason, I swear to you, I didn't –"

"I know you didn't," Jason assures him.

An agent steps in front of Nicholas. "Sir, this area is off limits –"

"This is private property, Officer. And considering the fact that you and your goons were parked on *my* property without my knowledge or permission, I demand to know what the hell you are arresting my friends for!"

"Obstruction of justice and evasion of the law. Now I suggest you shut up and fall back before I arrest you for aiding and abetting two fugitives!"

Nicholas looks between Jason and me. His eyes linger on Jason a little bit longer and I can only guess that Jason nods for him to leave. He backs away and the agent who spoke to him turns with a smug expression.

He walks up to me and says, "It didn't have to be like this, Nicolette. We could have worked something out at your parent's home –"

There's only one thing I want to know.

"Are you Agent Dannican?" I ask. He nods.

I kick my right leg up, long and strong. I catch him by the groin with the end of my shin. He immediately groans and doubles over in pain as the other agents pull me away.

"That's for my parents!"

Jason:

They separate us. I ignore the agents surrounding me and try to listen hard for any indication of where they're taking her. No one around me gives me any inkling. They take me to what looks like the local county jail and assign me to a single cell.

All I can think about as I lay here is where they might have taken her. I keep playing the look on her face as they cuffed her. The look she gave me when I promised her I would get her out of this. I know she didn't believe me. And why would she? I have no control of getting *myself* out of this mess, much less her.

I'm surprised they've given me my own cell. From what I overhear, the jail is so congested, I'm expecting an hour long wait before I can even get a mug shot.

Fortunately, that time never comes. About a half hour passes when I hear an all-too-familiar voice.

"Come on, son. Let's get out of here."

I turn on my cot and glare at McGrath. The guard standing beside him urges me out of the cell and takes me to a different station in the building. There, he gives me back my jacket and the keys to Dayjean's old Camry. I walk out of the building and find McGrath standing there with an impish expression.

"Forgive me?" he says.

"Go to hell," I bite back.

"Aww, come on son –"

"Don't call me that. Don't you ever call me that again. *I trusted you.* I trusted you and not only did you throw me under the bus, you hopped in the driver's seat!"

"We need her, Jason. Not just me. Not just Carter but the whole world *needs* her."

"You used me." It's not a question. He nods.

"Yes, I did. But I meant what I said. About caring for you."

I scoff.

"It's true," he insists. "If I didn't, I wouldn't have gone through all the trouble to have you pardoned."

"'Pardoned'? I did nothing wrong!" I shout.

"You did what you thought was right." He's trying to placate me. I begin to walk away from him. He follows me.

"The car is on the backside of the lot. They confiscated the weapons but I convinced them to leave the money and everything else. They'll also overlook you driving a vehicle that isn't legally registered to you."

Jesus. I know I just avoided a world full of legal trouble because of him but I can't get past what he's done.

"I had the back tires replaced," he says with a hopeful tone.

I keep walking.

"Jason, where are you going?"

I ignore him.

"Fine. Be mad at me. I deserve it!" he yells after me. "But don't try to interfere with her. You'll end up in trouble that even I can't get you out of."

That last statement makes me wonder... How was he able to get me released without charges? How was he able to get me my car, contents intact? He's an ER surgeon. How was he able to pull so many strings? And how did he get his hands on them in the first place?

I get a motel room and try figure out what to do. Surprisingly true to his word, all of Nic and my belongings are found intact, minus the weapons. The only gun I have left is the Glock I disassembled for the Disneyland trip. I reassemble it and place it on the night stand next to me. I call the crew at the shelter but they already know. Isaiah updates me.

"Dayjean got a call from the San Diego police department. I think they were hoping he'd say it was stolen."

"Ah, man. I don't want you guys getting sucked into this."

"No, it's fine. The vehicle is registered for Washington. This is out of their jurisdiction."

I let out a sigh of relief. But Isaiah isn't done.

"It's all over the news, Jason. They've locked her in a temporary holding facility. President Carter claims this is for her protection. "

"She's still in San Diego?"

"Yeah, so is the President. I talked to Eva. She says they're going to move her in two days. They want to secure samples from her to meet some of the demand first."

"Without her permission?" I ask incredulously.

"It's no longer in her hands."

I have to get her out of there. When I hang up with Isaiah, I give Eva a call. She's able to locate the facility they're holding Nic in and she pulls up a map of the framework as we talk. We spend the next two hours coming up with a plan.

"The only glitch is the doors," she says. "Jason, I can guarantee you each door has a pin pad, with a PIN specific to the employee working there. I don't have access to those PINs."

"We can't just shoot the locks?"

"Not without alerting every guard in the vicinity before we even get close to her."

I run my hand through my hair. It's the middle of the night and I am beyond exhausted. My stomach is empty and is tossing in turmoil - from fatigue, not hunger. I'm not thinking straight and it's as if she reads my mind.

"Look, get some rest and we'll figure this out later. I'll catch the first flight out of here," she says before hanging up.

I hit the sack and call it a night. I can feel myself begin to fade into the first lull of sleep when someone knocks on my door. I bolt out of my bed, load my pistol, and stand beside the door.

"Who is it?" I yell.

"Jason, it's Montgomery Norris. Please, I need to talk to you."

Nicolette:

I'm exhausted but they won't let me sleep. They take me to a nondescript building and pat me down for weapons. Several hands and metal detectors later and I'm ordered to follow two men in white lab coats to what looks like a phlebotomy room. They ask me to take a seat but I resist.

"Don't you need my permission to do this?"

One of the men looks down at his clipboard and reads:

"Executive Order 19187: RETRIEVE CURATIVE BLOOD FROM SOURCE REGARDLESS OF SOURCE'S APPROVAL."

My eyes widen in shock. I realize that I can either fight and lose or participate and hope that they won't draw more than is healthy for me. I sit and extend my preferred arm. They draw blood from both. To my relief they only draw a pint. It takes them a few minutes and they release me to the four waiting guards.

As I follow them to what I can only hope is a cell to sleep in, I feel like I'm in the twilight zone. The building can best be described as...sterile. All the walls, doors and tiled floors are white. Fluorescent lights beam down the long halls and there are several doors that practically blend into the walls beside them. Two guards walk ahead of me, two behind me. I almost feel a sense of pride that they feel the need to surround me so heavily, knowing that I can take on one, or even two, of them if given the chance.

They don't take me to a cell.

They cuff my hands once more and lead me into what looks like an interrogation room, fit with a metal table, two metal chairs, and one bright white light bulb hanging over the table. They seat me at the chair farthest from the door. About ten minutes later, I hear the distinct sound of clicking heels. The door opens and in walks President Brooklyn

Carter. Two secret service men walk in behind her but she holds up her hand and they retreat. The guard behind me leaves the room and closes the door. She sits in the metal chair opposite of me and stares.

Neither of us says a word.

Finally, she leans back in her seat and smirks.

"You really thought you could get away."

I ignore her. Why rise to the bait?

"I didn't want any of this to happen, you know. You running, your siblings in exile, your parents dead –"

"Don't." I warn her.

She narrows her eyes. "You miss them, don't you? You do realize that if you would have cooperated, none of this would have happened? Your parents would still be alive."

"You bitch." Her eyebrows shoot up in surprise. I continue, "You're the one who ordered the hit on my parents and you blame me? You lied to the public. There wasn't any sort of misunderstanding. You *planned* for them to die."

"I had to," she says matter-of-factly. "They weren't cooperating with me and I needed you. Nicolette, do you have any idea how much money is riding on your blood? *Six trillion dollars*. This is not about you."

"How do you sleep at night?"

"Time." She ignores me. "That's all I needed. Time and the world could be rid of disease and illness, pain and suffering-"

"Are you crazy? There is nothing that will completely expunge pain and suffering in this life-"

"At the very least our own country would be healthy." She shakes her head. "You surprise me. You could have had anything you wanted if you just said yes-"

"Anything but my freedom-"

"Freedom is overrated. Cash never is-"

"This was never about money for me."

"It's too bad you made the wrong choice. It's no longer your own now."

"This isn't legal," I remind her.

She shrugs. "No, it isn't. It's unprecedented. Never in a million years did I think Congress would grow a set and actually agree on something.

But they did! I'll be heading back to D.C. tonight to tie this up. Providing the cure for cancer can do wonders for your career."

I glare at her in disgust. "Shouldn't this be about helping the sick?"

"In theory. But in Washington, nothing is ever about what 'it's about.'"

"So what happened to 'honor' and 'sacrifice?'"

She rolls her eyes. "Nicolette, I am a politician, not a philanthropist. Anything I said to you that night was to get what I needed. And now I have it."

She stands.

"Get some rest. McGrath and the others will draw samples tomorrow." With that said, she turns around and leaves.

The guards finally take me to my sleeping quarters, which consists of nothing more than a small bed, standalone sink, and small latrine. They shut the door and lock it but I can see the feet of two guards standing by the door.

Now that I'm in a place where I can finally rest, all I can think about is Jason and what he said at the park.

"Did you ever stop to think that maybe you have this blood for a reason?"

Well now I have the time to stop and think about it. I think about my conversation with Isaiah and what he said about God. If there is a God and he made me and everything else on this planet, why did he give me this blood? What does he want me to do with it?

CHAPTER FOURTEEN

Jason:

"What do you want?" I ask in a hostile tone. "What are you even *doing* here?"

Norris looks at me with a pleading expression. He looks around him and lowers his voice.

"Can I please come in?"

"No," I snap. "What do you want?"

"I want to help you."

I narrow my eyes at him and survey him skeptically. I step aside and let him in. I close the door, turn to face him and find him pacing the room. He glances at the gun in my hand.

"Jason, I had nothing to do with them finding you."

"That doesn't mean I trust you."

"I get it. You're pissed. But I want you to know I had no idea how deep McGrath was into this."

"What do you mean?"

"He's been working with President Carter since day one."

What?

He reads the confusion on my face and continues.

"McGrath knew about the potential of Nicolette's blood from the beginning. He alerted Carter and struck a deal with her before anyone else could."

I think of all the strings he pulled for me. *No wonder.* It all makes sense. But I still don't get why he's here.

"I was genuinely excited about her blood. About finding the cure and helping people but McGrath asked me to be the pusher, the one sticking my hands in everything so that he could look trustworthy to you and I would be the bad guy."

"Why did you do it?" I ask. "What does McGrath have on you?"

"My C-K in med school. During the second step, I...I was less than honest when taking it. McGrath knew I was struggling to retain the information so he introduced me to a friend of his who helped me through the test. So I owed him one...and he threatened to tell everyone about it unless I helped him."

"You said you came here to help me."

"I did. I have to play along with McGrath but it doesn't mean I can't help the other team behind his back."

That's when he pulls out a folded sheet from his coat pocket. He opens it up: it's a map with several five digit codes, each assigned to a doorway in the map.

The PINs.

"Nicolette is in 319."

"They might trace this back to you, you know?" I warn him.

He nods. "I know the risks."

I extend my hand.

"Thank you."

He shakes it and nods. "Is there any other way I can help you?"

"Actually, there is."

Nicolette:

The next day goes by excruciatingly slow. They take more samples of my blood and feed me iron tablets to help replenish my blood count. They then ask me very detailed questions about my health background, my family ancestry, and bring in a nutritionist to guarantee the best supply of blood. They inform me that I'll be transferred to a different facility tomorrow morning but they don't specify where. I hate it here. The people are cold and taciturn. They don't even try to pretend that they're remotely interested in me or my well-being. Everything is about my blood.

They escort me back to my "room" at the end of the day and I hit the sack. I can't stop thinking about Jason. Is he locked up somewhere? Are they giving him hell for helping me? I wish I could see him. I try to remember his voice, his smile, the warmth of his hug. Tomorrow I'll be God-only-knows where, even more removed from him. I almost feel like praying but I don't even know how. A thought escapes my mind like a leaf caught in the wind.

Help me. I want to help other people but not for a price. Help me help others without the interference of these leeches. If you exist, please help me.

Next Morning - 2:00 AM

Jason:

We pull up to a dark alley, one block of the facility in a large white van Norris rented for us. He helms the wheel while Eva and I prepare in the back. We both pull on bullet-protective vests and load our ammunition: guns, mace, and a couple of knives. Eva stuffs a couple of grenade-looking balls into her vest.

She opens the hatch door of the van, perfectly positioned above a sewer drain top. She pulls on a pair of black gloves, takes a dark spray bottle and sprays the perimeter of the sewer top with some sort of chemical. The chemical foams and hisses and smoke rises from the top. She reaches down and pops the top off like a hat box.

I turn to Norris and hand him a gun. His eyes look like clocks in his small round head.

I tell him, "If we're not out by five—"

"Four –" Eva interrupts.

"—four, you leave. Got it?"

He nods and clears his throat. "Be careful, Jason."

We tread through the dark, putrid sewer with flashlights on. It takes us almost half an hour to make our way to the tunnel of the facility. We reach a ladder to the landing of the building. I climb first and enter the

PIN Norris gave me. The locks pop open and we're in. We're in the stairwell of the building. We run up the stairs and onto the third level.

Once there, I peek through the window of the door and sure enough there is a guard pacing back and forth in front of it. I enter the next PIN and the lock pops. The guard whips around and stops. I open the door just slightly as Eva takes one of the grenade-balls and unclasps it before rolling it down the hall towards the man. The place soon fills with fog and the man runs over to the door.

That's when I move.

I slam through — propelling the door against his groin. He yelps in pain — bounces on the back of his heels. He reaches for his gun but I quickly catch his arm. I yank him towards Eva and she handles him like a ragdoll, snapping his other arm with a clean hand jab.

"Ahh!" he yells out. Eva quickly covers his mouth and in a smooth motion, twists his neck until a clean pop is heard. The man falls unconscious. She turns to me.

"The fog will only last twenty minutes. If we don't want these," she points to the security cameras, "to pick us up, we have to move."

We run down the hallway and turn left. The building is like a maze but we've studied it and run confidently. *305, 307, 309...* We make a right. *311, 313, 315...*

"FREEZE!" we hear behind us. We run even faster.

"FREEZE!" they repeat. "Freeze or we will fire!"

Eva stops and I look at her. She turns around slowly and lifts her hands above her head. The guards run closer to us.

"What are you doing?" I hiss.

She whispers, "When I say…"

The guards keep their weapons up.

Guard One yells, "Jake, check her."

One of the men emerges from the fog as he approaches Eva cautiously. We can't see them clearly but from their outline, I can tell the other two keep their guns drawn. He is about to pat her when suddenly – she's in motion. She swiftly turns the guard around in a vice neck grip, while simultaneously drawing her gun.

"Run!" she yells at me.

I take off while she holds the guard hostage. I play the map in my head and follow it the best I can, the fog making it difficult to see. I make a second left and then a right before I see more rooms. I can hear my feet hit the waxed tile, my breath panting as I run. I also hear commotion behind me, which must be Eva and the guards. Shots ring and I suddenly hear Eva.

"Ahh!" she yells in pain.

I don't stop. I pull out my gun; turn one more hall and bam – room 319 at the end of it. Two guards stand there, guns drawn in anticipation. Guard One sees me and points his gun at me.

"Freeze!"

I look up at the fluorescent lights above me. It's one extremely long panel that lights the hallway.

"Raise your hands where we can see them!" Guard Two shouts.

The problem is they really can't see me. My outline maybe, but not much else. I lift my left hand up but keep the right behind my back.

"Both hands! Now!"

Nicolette:

Something wakes me up. I stir in my bed and turn towards the door. There's shouting right outside of it. Feet shuffle in front of it and I hear someone yell:

"We're not going to tell you again-"

"Both hands – NOW!"

Jason:

It's now or never. I pull my right arm, gun in hand and drop to the ground as the Guard One shoots. He shoots too high and misses me but I don't miss. I catch him in the knee with one shot —

"Ahhh!"

—then shoot the fluorescent panel above me. All the lights immediately go out. I can hear the second guard panic as he radios for help.

"Code two! Code two! In need of immediate assistance –"

Nicolette:

Something is wrong. I thought Carter was full of it when she said there were others out to get me but now I'm not so sure. I bolt out of my bed when I hear shots ring. One of the guards yells out and sinks to the floor. The other guard yells in his radio for back up but doesn't even finish his sentence before grunting in pain. I see the shadow of his body slump to the ground. Another shadow stands right beside it.

Right beside my door.

I look around in panic. The mirror! I pull on my sneakers, kick the mirror with my heel and pull a sharp shard of glass. I run next to the door, back flat against the wall. The locks pop and the door opens; I see his outline and I lunge but he catches my wrist and twists it in a hold. I cry out in pain and he immediately lets go of me.

"Nic, it's me."

"Jason?"

Relief floods my senses as I turn and pull him into my arms. He pulls back just enough to look me over and asks in concern, "Are you okay?"

I rub my wrist. "I am now. How did you find me?"

"I told you I would get you."

"I know, but how-"

"Excuse me, but this is not the time to be conversing."

It's Eva. She stands outside the door with a flashlight in hand and a grin on her face. Now I know how he did it. I run over to her and give her huge hug. She winces involuntarily and pulls back. I look down and gasp. There's a gaping wound in her thigh.

"I'm fine," she says. "Let's go."

CHAPTER FIFTEEN

Jason:

We make our way back to the sewer relatively easily. Ignoring her protests, I carry Eva the entire way and continue to carry her through the dark damp, passage as Nic follows closely.

"How you doing?" I ask Eva.

"Okay," she grunts.

"Hang on, Eva." Nic says.

"Yeah, we're almost there."

Eva rolls her eyes and says exasperatedly, "It's just a flesh wound. I'm not dying here!"

"SPLIT UP! FOUR TEAMS IN EACH DIRECTION!" we hear a male voice shout. We stop in our tracks and look back. There are other flashlights bouncing off the damp walls behind us.

"We have to move," Eva says. I look down at her and she nods. We both know what needs to happen. I place her gently back on her feet and she wraps her arm around Nic.

"You guys keep going," I tell them.

Nic's not happy. "Jason, what are you –"

"Don't argue with me, Nic. Just go. Eva knows the way back."

"Jason –"

Eva cuts her off. "There's no time. Come on."

She reluctantly pulls Eva forward. I turn, re-load my gun, and head towards the guards.

Nicolette:

"Okay," Eva says. "We're here."

I climb up the ladder and reach what looks like a hatch door. I bang on it.

"Who is it?" a muffled voice yells.

I look down at Eva and she nods.

"Nicolette! Please, hurry up!"

The hatch opens and the last person I expected opens it.

"Dr. Norris!" I feel such an overwhelming urge to retract from the man that I literally begin to climb back down the ladder.

"Nikki, it's okay." Eva says. "He's helping us."

He extends his hand to me. I look down at her and she nods again. I reach up, take his hand and he pulls me through. Seconds later, he pulls Eva through, closes the hatch and begins to treat her wound. I want to ask why Eva and Jason think him trustworthy because all I can remember is him constantly pushing me and my parents for more during the research trials.

But there are more important things to worry about – like Eva's injury. And Jason.

"Where is he?" Dr. Norris asks.

Jason:

I press my back into the sewer wall as I listen to the damp footsteps draw closer. I'm right at the edge of the wall and I can see the guards' shadows grow bigger and bigger. There are three of them.

"I don't hear them anymore," one says.

I can feel the adrenaline pulsing through my blood.

"They probably got away," says another.

I take deep breaths, trying to rein my nerves in.

"It doesn't matter. We still have to look."

They reach my corner and I move.

Nicolette:

I hold the flashlight to Eva's wound as Dr. Norris examines it. Eva puts on a brave face but I can tell she's in a great deal of pain. Not to mention the fact that she's lost a lot of blood. She's drenched in sweat and is panting harder than before. He flushes out the wound with antibiotics and packs it with gauze.

He stands and says, "Well, it looks like the bullet went through you. There's no trace of it in or around your wound."

"Yay, no surgery," she pants out.

"We managed to get the bleeding to stop but you have already lost a lot of blood. This isn't a fix. I'm only a hematologist. Jason's going to have to look at it."

"Speaking of Jason," Eva says. "Where the hell is he?"

"I don't know," he says, glancing at his watch. "But it's 4:05. He specifically said –"

"We're not leaving," I cut him off.

"Nicolette, you barely got out of there," he reasons. "Eva still needs to be seen by someone and Jason told me in no uncertain terms to leave –"

"We are *not* leaving him behind!"

"He has twenty minutes," Eva says firmly. "If he's not here, we're going."

I open my mouth to protest.

"*Twenty minutes*, Nicolette."

"You don't understand," he says. He turns to Eva. "You might not *have* twenty minutes."

I roll up my sleeves and stick out my left arm.

Eva looks from me to him.

"I do now."

He draws my blood and gives it to her. Within minutes, she stops sweating and her breathing returns to normal. I can see from the look on her face that she's no longer in pain.

"Thank you," she whispers to me.

"Thank *you*," I whisper back.

It's 4:10. I watch the clock and wish that I could slow down time. Minute by minute rushes forth and still he hasn't shown up. Suddenly, we hear a loud ring of shots below, followed by footsteps running in the sewer right beneath us.

"Jason!" I exclaim. I reach to open the hatch but Eva stops me and loads her gun.

"What if it's not him?"

"What if it is?" I retort.

Someone knocks on the hatch. Eva points her gun at the closed door and nods at Dr. Norris. He kneels by it and yells out.

"Who is it?"

The knock becomes more insistent, as if someone is pursuing the person. It must be Jason. He probably knows he's late and is trying to reach us.

"This is ridiculous." I reach forward and unlock the hatch.

"Nikki, no!"

It's too late.

To my shock and utter horror, up pops a man I've never seen in my life. He's in uniform and only inches away from me. Eva shoots him in the shoulder –

"Ahh!"

—but not before he grabs my arm and pulls me through the hatch opening. I feel myself catapult forward but Dr. Norris manages to catch my legs. I feel Eva pull me up by the waist but the guard has a firm grip on my wrist. I struggle to break free with my other arm but he won't let go.

Another shot rings and this time I feel a vibration shoot up my arm. I look down and see red fluid spread through the center of his chest. A shot goes off again, this time through the torso. His grip loosens, his hands release me and he falls, past the ladder, and into the damp, wet sewer below. A shadow approaches the body and I begin to retreat.

"I told you to leave at four."

"Jason!"

He climbs up, gun in hand and I throw myself into his arms. He squeezes me tight, pulls back and looks at Eva.

"You okay?"

She opens her mouth to respond when, suddenly, we're all violently jostled as Dr. Norris speeds off, tires squealing.

"Close the hatch!"

Jason:

Norris drives like a lunatic. I'm grateful on two scores: that he doesn't kill us and that we make it to the border in under an hour. We're able to pass through on the visas Eva prepared for us and we make it to *Punta Banderas* unscathed. We pull up to a small, obviously private, lot full of jets. It's still early in the morning and the sun is about to rise when we manage to charter a plane from a Mexican man in his mid-forties who speaks broken English.

We load the plane with our stuff and turn to bid Eva and Norris farewell.

"Thank you," Nic says. "Thank you both so much."

"Anytime," Eva smiles.

"Never again," Norris says simultaneously.

We all laugh as our bodies come off the adrenaline rush. Eva reaches into her back pocket and pulls out two passports. We flip them open and find our pictures inside; mine, next to the name "Dr. Oliver Smith," hers next to "Jennifer Dawson."

"Just in case," she says.

I pull her into my arms, kiss her cheek, and whisper.

"Thank you."

She pulls back and smiles. Nicolette hands her a wad of cash.

"For your expenses...and Harvest Hope. Also..." Nicolette turns from all of us and reaches into her shirt. She holds out the tiny cashew-shaped piece of metal for Eva. "This did come in handy. Please make sure this gets heard."

Eva nods and they embrace.

"Take care of yourself," she glances at me, "and him."

I roll my eyes, extend my hand to Norris and thank him again. We say our last goodbyes and head for the plane. We're all strapped in and ready to take off but I don't let it seep in that we've managed to get away until the wheels are safely off the land. I hear Nic sigh next to me and I know she feels the same way.

"We made it," I tell her. She doesn't respond and when I look at her, I can see tears welling in her eyes.

"What?" I ask.

"You came back for me," she whispers.

"I told you I would."

"Jason. People don't come back for me."

"I do." I answer firmly. "I see you, Nicolette."

She looks up at me and says in a really frustrated tone, "What's happening here?"

Wow. She totally just put me on the spot and I have to admit that I'm flustered by it. Just when I'm about to respond she speaks again.

"I like you."

"That's all you feel?"

She looks down at her hands.

"What's it to you? You obviously don't feel the same," she snaps.

"You're right. I don't feel the same."

Her eyes widen as if I just slapped her in the face.

"I don't feel the same way because I don't just 'like' you," I explain. "I love you."

I can't really describe what it feels like to tell a girl you love her for the first time. Nor can I describe the look in her eyes the second I admit it. Everything softens in her liquid hazel gaze and something much deeper than tenderness fills them. Once again we lean closer to each other as if our very eyes are magnets.

And in some random charter plane, flying over some random part of the world: we kiss.

Brooklyn:

"There's no trace of them. They could be miles away from us at this point."

"How did this happen, Kennedy?"

"McGrath, I wasn't on the scene."

"You never are!"

"Stop arguing with me and help me track her down. If you hadn't had that kid released, none of this would be happening."

"We don't know who helped her escape –"

"Jason Monroe is nowhere to be seen. Admit it, he's behind this…"

The two men continue to argue but I can't hear them. Neither can I hear Agent Dannican and his men as they rush into my office and try to give me the latest report. The phone rings and I know it's Elizabeth Shune, wanting to know how we'll handle the news of her escape. A White House Aid enters and tells me several ambassadors are on hold for me. I turn my chair and face the window behind me. Everything is crashing around me and I didn't even see it coming.

"Well played, kid." I whisper into the morning. "Well played."

CHAPTER SIXTEEN

Nicolette:

I'm keenly aware that I must look like Julia Roberts out of *The Pelican Brief* as I lounge in my beach chair. The waves lick the sand behind me and retreat back to their warm depths. I sip my lemonade through a straw, and roll the sweet liquid over my tongue. My eyes are plastered to the rickety TV screen that sits before me. I hear my voice play as CNN airs captions of an old conversation.

"You're the one who ordered the hit on my parents and you blame me? You lied to the public. There wasn't any sort of misunderstanding. You planned for them to die."

"I had to. They weren't cooperating with me and I needed you. Nicolette, do you have any idea how much money is riding on your blood? Six trillion dollars. This is not about you."

They've edited the conversation to highlight her most egregious statements.

"Freedom is overrated. Cash never is. Never in a million years did I think Congress would grow a set and actually agree on something. But they did! Providing the cure for cancer can do wonders for your career."

"Shouldn't this be about helping the sick?"

"In theory. But in Washington, nothing is ever about what 'it's about.'"

"So what happened to 'honor' and 'sacrifice?'"

"Nicolette, I am a politician, not a philanthropist. Anything I said to you that night was to get what I needed. And now I have it."

The screen cuts to a black male reporter.

"As of this broadcast, Nicolette Talloway's whereabouts are still unknown. Kennedy Tyler, White House chief of staff, has resigned and President Carter has made it clear that she will not run for another term. Human rights activists, however, are still crying for the President's impeachment by reason of perjury and murder, with most of the nation reeling over the discovery of President Carter's direct involvement with Thomas and Stacy Talloway's deaths."

Footage of protesters with picket signs flash across the screen. I pick up one that says: "You drove her out of here." "Aggression cost us the cure." "Killer cover-up." "Presidential murder!"

"Polls have indicated that no president has been this unpopular since George W. Bush. Dr. Greg McGrath declined to comment in the aftermath of his recent termination from Wakefield Memorial Hospital."

I finish my lemonade and head over to the hut nearby, the TV still on. The sign above it reads in *Sinhala*: "Hospital of Christ." Inside, I find Jason wrapping a little boy's wrist with gauze. He speaks to him in *Sinhala* but the boy answers in English.

"Much better. Thank you, Doctor."

Jason gives the kid a lollipop and ruffles his hair. The kid jumps off the table and runs past me and out of the hut. I turn from watching him and find Jason's eyes lit on me, a tender smile on his face. He pulls me into a warm, masculine hug and we listen to the newsreel play on.

"Miss Talloway's siblings remain in exile in France. Neither have disclosed their sister's whereabouts despite constant speculation that they are fully aware of it. Samples of Miss Talloway's blood have mysteriously appeared at labs, hospitals, and universities around the world with no trace of the original sender. St. Jude's is currently the most heavily received benefactor in the United States and France is the one of the highest benefactors in the world, second to countries in West Africa."

"You sent the latest batch?" I ask in his ear.

"Mm-hmm."

"Authorities believe Miss Talloway may still be on the run with accomplice, Dr. Jason Monroe."

"Umm, we're not running!" Jason scoffs.

"'Accomplice.' If only they knew."

He pulls back and looks down at me, digs his hand in my shoulder-length hair and pulls my mouth to his own. This kiss is deep and sound and I revel in the soft touch of his lips. He pulls back and whispers:

"If only they knew."

To be continued...

Author's Note

Dear Reader:

I want to thank you for taking the time to read my debut novel, *Type N*. While this isn't the first book I've written, it is definitely the first full-length novel I've endeavored to write.

You might wonder how I came up with the idea for the premise and I have to admit it was from something as simple as finding out what my blood type was. I was always curious and for some reason the hospital where I was born didn't have it on record so I paid to find out.

As I was looking over my results and thinking on the different blood types that are known, the premise for this book really came out of a "What if?" thought. What if someone had a blood type that didn't fit in any of the known categories? What if she had her own blood type that no one else on earth did? And what if her blood could do really cool things, like cure other diseases? And alas, *Type N* was conceived.

I hope you enjoyed the story and I do hope you'll take the time to write a review and let me and other readers know what you thought of the book. **The sequel** for *Type N* is now available, and the first chapter of the book follows. Please keep in touch and join my Facebook page to stay in the loop (www.facebook.com/authormichelleonuorah). Please also feel free to explore my other work via my Amazon page or my website: www.michelleonuorah.webs.com.

Also, if you are a non-believer and are curious to learn more about Christ, please feel free to contact me. I'm more than glad to share :)

Sincerely,
Michelle

TAKING NAMES

CHAPTER ONE

Moscow, Russia – 12:00 PM

Nicolette:

My left shoulder is sore. I'm worried that I've broken a bone or wrenched a socket in the landing. I need to get out of here. Shortly after my insane jump, the truck exits the freeway and pulls into a busy shopping center. As he drives through an outside parking lot, I climb out of the cab, hang off the end of the truck and jump off. It drives on. I get strange glances from strangers but by some miracle, the driver doesn't detect me.

My shoulder is on fire now and my whole arm feels numb. Something is wrong. I rush into what looks like a convenience store and immediately catch the attention of the employees there. They don't say anything but they look at me strangely, not in recognition but concern at my pained expression and the way I'm gripping my arm. I probably look disheveled too.

"First aid," I say in Russian. One of the reps points to aisle four. I stride to it, pull the first kit I find, tuck it under my right arm and quickly slam more than enough money on the counter top with my right hand. I turn to the bathroom at the back of the store before the attendants can even speak. The minute I close the door, I strip off my backpack, jacket, and shirt. First things first. I place a firm hand on my left shoulder, take a deep breath and wrench it back into place. The pain is blinding and the shock of it knocks the breath out of me. My gasps fill the bathroom. Whatever relief I feel in having my shoulder back in place is suspended when I look at it in the mirror. Immediately, I see another problem.

There is something implanted in my shoulder and dried blood has streaked from the entry site. I push and prod at it and then realize – it's a *bullet.* I've never seen this before and feel like the subject of a strange sci-fi show. The dried streak of blood around my wound indicates that I bled but only briefly. The wound is closed around the bullet. My skin stitched itself back together over a wound that would ordinarily require stitches at the least. But I can't leave it like that. Even if I don't get an infection from the foreign object, the feel of it there is incredibly uncomfortable.

I have to get it out.

I wash my hands, open the kit, pull on gloves, and immediately go for the scalpel. I sterilize it then force myself to do what I would normally find nauseating. I swallow my fear and dig the edge of the blade into my skin. Ignoring the blood, I cut a small circle around the edge of the bullet, and dig into the new opening. I dig and push as blood streams past my shoulder and onto my chest. The tip of the blade makes contact with the bullet. I pry it out and hear it clink into the bowl of the sink. I check around the burrow of the wound for any shrapnel pieces. It's clear. Red but clear. I bite my lip and hold back a scream as I sterilize the wound with alcohol, pack it with gauze, and seal it with tape. I hope it will close on its own again. Otherwise, the stitching will have to wait.

I've got to get out of here.

I toss the contents of the rudimentary surgery away and clean myself up. My clothes are ruined with blood and I think that's what alarmed the employees the most. I change tops but wear the same jacket.

As I emerge from the bathroom, I can tell something is up. There are whispers in Russian. I walk down an aisle concealing myself from sight of the employees at the front desk. Through cans of shaving cream and deodorant, I see them. Three men in *politsiya* uniforms. I don't have time for this. I walk to the end of the aisle and make myself visible. The three men straighten and I see recognition flash in their eyes. One pulls his radio to his mouth. The other says, "Excuse me, ma'am," in Russian. I ignore him and turn into another aisle. I hear their feet scatter. I stride down one aisle and hear them stride down the one parallel to me on my left. I glance at the corner ceilings and, just as I expected, find large mirrors stationed on every corner of the building. I grab a can of what appears to be hair spray and pop off the cap. Stand at the end of the aisle and watch as one of the men bound down to my direction.

"Aminev," a *politsiya* suddenly yells in warning. He's seen the mirror and so does my target. Aminev reaches for his gun but I'm quicker. I knock his hand with the edge of my foot, strike the side of his head with my forearm and stomp my foot in my favorite place on the knee. He crumples to the ground and I quickly disarm him. I hold my hand steady and shoot out the mirrors. First one, then another, until all four are blown out. I barely hear the screams of customers as they race out of the building in a mad dash. I yank up Aminev by his uniform and plant the barrel of my gun into his dark hair.

His partners have no choice but to face me. Their guns drawn, they see they're at a disadvantage as their comrade lies in clear hostage. They come from separate corners but I can see them both. I look at the cop on my left and gesture to the cop on the right.

"Join him," I command in Russian. His eyebrows shoot up in surprise at my use of the language. He slowly moves to join the other officer.

I'm calling the shots now.

Kuchchaveli Beach, Sri Lanka – Five Weeks Earlier:

I breathe deep. Hold the breath and feel the rush of liquid as I submerge beneath the water. It's still. Warm at the surface, cool down below. The sun beams forth, warming my face. It's nothing compared to the warmth in my heart. Time stands still under that water and all I hear is liquid silence. Peace below. I meet Him in the deep and it blows my mind that centuries ago, He did the very same thing. He leaned back into the water, His back held by His cousin. He broke through the water and felt the sun dance off the droplets on His face. This isn't just a ritual. Or a ceremony. It's a celebration. Of the life I have in Him. My God. My Christ. My baptism.

I break through the water. The cheers are overwhelming. No dove descends and the sky doesn't part but I know that He is pleased. I know I am His child. I believe that Jesus Christ is all that he claimed to be and I know that He lives. I don't know exactly when I started to believe. I think maybe I always did - even as a kid. But I didn't know how to connect with Him until Isaiah and Jason showed me how. And I didn't admit it until Jason asked.

I open my eyes and look at Jason. The man who introduced me to my Savior. The man who gave up everything to keep me safe. The man who told me he loved me just hours after we escaped. There are tears in his dark blue eyes but they come from nothing short of joy. Nothing short of love. Finally, we can be one. Our new beginning is limitless.

Jason:

This has to be the most unusual baptism-wedding to ever take place. The fact that it's a baptism-wedding is strange in and of itself.

And yet it's right.

When Nic breaks through the water, a joy and a peace so potent overtakes us all. I cheer, Pastor Thennakoon cheers and so do the members of his small congregation - our fellow Brothers and Sisters. There are no more than six people in the water with us. She turns to me immediately and I wrap her up in my arms, soaking right along with her. I think back to the lonely, sullen teenager I first met nearly three years ago. When she was dressed in nothing but black and had no one to call friend. She has transformed. Always beautiful, God's light shines in her and through her. Her jet black hair glistens in the sun and her skin glows with a healthy tan. Her cheeks are flushed with excitement. Her smile is radiant and it makes her all the more beautiful to me.

One year. More than a year, actually.

It's been more than a year since I first told Nic I loved her on that charter plane. I have waited - honoring her with my patience; refusing to push her into anything she wasn't ready for: a deeper relationship with me, which would only happen with a deeper relationship with God. She accepted Christ into her heart only months after we arrived in Sri Lanka but she waited to get baptized. And I waited to propose. The baptism is over. I'm ready for the wedding.

We turn to face the pastor. We're both drenched in water as we stand waist deep in the sea. She wears a simple white dress and I match her with a simple white collared shirt. My khakis cling to my legs under water but I don't mind. Pastor Thennakoon reaches to one of the congregants and they pass him a leather-back Bible. He's careful to hold it high above the water as he reads:

"'A man will leave his father and mother and be united to his wife, and they will become one flesh.' We are gathered here today to join this man and this woman into holy matrimony under the witness and blessing of God."

He says it again in *Sinhala*.

Nic and I join hands. We're still drenched. There's no makeup, no videographer, no frills or thrills associated with the typical Western wedding. But it doesn't matter. We're not in the West and we no longer need the frills. There is love; our love for each other and more importantly, our love for the One uniting us. She's radiant - more beautiful to me than she ever was before. We exchange the vows in English but speak very low. So low that only Pastor Thennakoon can hear what we're saying:

"I, Jason Dockery Monroe, take you, Nicolette Jennifer Talloway, to be my lawfully wedded wife. To have and to hold from this day forward, for better or worse, for richer or poorer, in sickness and in health."

Tears flow freely down her cheeks as I meet her eyes and pledge my life to her.

"I vow to love, honor, and cherish you. In the name of Jesus Christ, I commit my heart and my body to you and to our marriage and I pledge to you my fidelity until death do us part."

Our rings are simple golden bands - hers, slim and feminine; mine, slightly thicker. I slip hers on and kiss it as it beams brightly on her hand.

A smile breaks through the tears as she squeezes my hands and mouths "I love you." I immediately mouth it back.

It's her turn.

She takes a deep breath and steadies herself. Meets my eyes again and begins:

"I, Nicolette Jennifer Talloway, take you, Jason Dockery Monroe, to be my lawfully wedded husband. To have and to hold from this day forward, for better or worse, for richer or poorer." Her voice breaks and she pauses, tears gushing forth again. My own have long since fallen.

She continues, "In sickness and in health. I vow to love, honor, and cherish you. In the name of Jesus Christ, I commit my heart and my body to you and our marriage. I pledge to you my fidelity until death do us part."

She slips the band on my finger and I look at it. I raise my eyes to hers and am held hostage by her eyes.

We're all silent for a moment. We hear nothing but the waves as the words sink in to both of us - the commitment we just made to one another - that we'll hold ourselves to for the rest of our lives. I'm not afraid. I've been ready for so long. All I feel is a happiness I never thought I could feel. Suddenly, Pastor Thennakoon's voice booms out in *Sinhala*:

"I now pronounce you Mr. and Mrs. Oliver Smith!"

The church cheers and claps as Pastor Thennakoon smiles mischievously at us. He's the only one who knows, the only one we've trusted enough to tell and he's kept our confidence for the past year. All of our documents read "Dr. Oliver Smith" and "Jennifer Dawson." Even the marriage license we filed yesterday. In the eyes of the church members, the public, and the Sri Lankan government, Nic and I are two people who don't really exist. We can let it bother us or we can accept it as a price to pay for our freedom. Besides, God knows the truth. The vows that we just gave were the truth. Pastor Thennakoon knows this too. He looks at us and whispers in English:

"I now pronounce you Dr. and Mrs. Jason Monroe." He looks at me. "You may kiss your lovely bride."

I turn my focus back to her and all I can see are her hazel eyes. They're glowing with elation, love, and a fearless anticipation for the life we have ahead of us. I pull Nic flush into my arms, cradle her gently at the nape of her neck and lower my mouth to hers. The cheers from the crowd thunder in my ears as we kiss. Her lips are soft, wet, and inviting. I get so lost in the moment it takes me a second to realize we're not alone.

"Hey, hey - save some for your wedding night!" Pastor Thennakoon teases in *Sinhala*. The crowd roars in laughter.

I pull back blushing but Nic just laughs. She catches my eye and begins to sober.

We're married.

Nicolette:

Finally.

I have been waiting for this night for so long. The reception is over, Pastor Thennakoon and the rest of our guests have gone home. The sun is just setting as Jason and I stand in what was once his room. For over a year we've lived in separate small beach houses only yards away from each other, right by the water. Jason had been intent on finding separate homes that wouldn't lend us to compromising his values; values that soon became mine.

But that season is over. We're married now. And our homes will now converge into one.

We face each other. It's times like this that I can't get past how beautiful he is. It's like God was in a really good mood the day He made him and rather than just painting a decent picture, He decided to create a masterpiece out of him. The setting sun casts a warm orange-pink glow on the side of my new husband's face. His hair is blonder than it ever was. He keeps it cropped but it's longer than it was in the States and is tousled from the day's activities. I blush to think how much more tousled it's about to get. The shadows cast by the mellow sun sharpen the angles of his high cheekbones, chiseled jaw, and perfect straight nose. But it's his eyes...his eyes give me chills. The dark blue set against the warm orange glow of the sun. And they're fixed on me with a look I've only glimpsed once or twice in all our time together. They're hungry with an intensity that makes my senses swim.

He desires me.

And I desire him.

I slowly kick off the sandals on my feet. Remove the bangle from my wrist and let it drop to the floor with a careless thud. Finally, I remove the straps of my dress. It falls to a puddle at my feet. I hear his sharp intake of breath. He echoes my movements. Removes his sandals, his shirt and his pants. We stand in front of each other, only covered by underwear. I'm barely aware of the breath that comes out as a gasp. What's wrong with me? I've seen magazine covers and movie posters before. I've seen shirtless actors with ripped bodies. Heck, I've seen Jason without his shirt on before, swimming at the beach. But there's something different about seeing Jason shirtless before me right now, in this moment. Knowing that his body, taut with muscle, is for me and me alone. I look back up into his eyes and see the same look of awe reflected back at me. His breath has accelerated and is quicker than my own.

He steps forward. Takes my hand and places it on his warm chest in invitation. I accept it and allow my hands to explore the planes of his hard muscled chest, shoulders, biceps, and torso. I can feel his heart racing. He feels so strong, almost imposing as he towers over me. The thought of being intimate with him is almost intimidating. He must read it on my face.

"Don't be afraid. I'll be gentle."

I smile up at him, at his look of concern for me.

"I know you will," I reply.

I take his hands and bring them to my waist in invitation. He steps closer and caresses my back and shoulders. He looks down at me, cherishing me, assessing my readiness. I meet his eyes and nod. He lowers his mouth to mine and kisses all the thoughts away. Kisses me until I hardly notice when we reach the bed. Kisses me until it barely registers that all our clothes are gone.

He is gentle.

And patient. He's a selfless lover and I'm the beneficiary. And though my body feels the pain of him taking my virginity, it thrills me to see the pleasure register on his face. He doesn't let it cloud him from focusing on me. He watches me closely, his dark blue eyes gauging my expression as he loves me tenderly. And as he loves me tenderly, the pain recedes to the background and a new pleasure springs forth. Our breaths mingle as we give, we take, and we enjoy our union. He makes me his wife and I make him my husband.

Our covenant is consummated. We've finally become one.

Jason:

My body burned with a thirst only she could quench. And she's quenched it. The only flame that's left in me is one that settles deep in my heart. I love her. I love her so much it almost hurts. Her hand strokes my chest and my hands caress her arms. We've made love all night but can't seem to stop touching each other. I'm finding that the more I make love to her, the deeper the love in my heart takes root. And the deeper that love takes root, the more I'm compelled to make love to her. It's a cycle that I really don't mind.

We lie in the pool of sheets and allow the breeze of the night to cool our bodies. We're satisfied. My joints feel like liquid as I stare up at the wood-beamed ceiling. Nic's jet black hair fans out over my arm as I hold her close to me. She kisses my chest and smiles up at me.

"Love you," I whisper.

"Love you, too."

She stretches out across me and threatens to arouse me again. Fortunately, we're both too tired. She readjusts herself and sits up on one elbow, looking down at me this time.

"I'm scared," she says suddenly. I frown at her questioningly.

"I'm scared that this is too perfect. That we're too happy."

I nod. I know exactly what she means.

"It's been over a year," I point out. "If they were going to find us, don't you think they'd do it within weeks of our arrival here?"

I think back to our journey. The road trip, the brush at Disneyland, the time we got caught and were almost separated forever. If it weren't for Eva, Norris, and the crew, we would still be in the States; Nic, a lab rat for the government and me, a hired hand for literally siphoning her blood.

I shudder at the thought. She reads my face and nods.

"We're better here."

In the time Nic and I have made our new home in Sri Lanka, we have donated enough samples of her blood to cure a small country. My practice has flourished but as a rule, I never use her blood to treat my patients. We send the blood out but don't let it play a role in our lives. While I practice medicine, ministering to my patients in *Sinhala*, she practices her art, selling her pieces to local vendors who in turn sell them to tourists and other art lovers. On every painting, sketch, and sculpture, she simply signs "John 3:16" instead of her name. She amazes me.

"Do you forgive them?" I ask. The question pops out of my mouth before it fully develops in my head. I'm not sure why I ask or even that I care. But I watch her all the same. The expression in her hazel eyes alters just slightly.

"Do you?" she replies.

I frown. "Their hunt didn't do anything to me, Nic. They were always after you."

She shakes her head. "Not them. Your parents. Do you forgive your parents?"

Now I understand. She's deflecting.

"I forgave them a long time ago."

Her eyes widen. She's surprised.

"Do you know how long I've been praying for you?" I ask.

She frowns. "Praying for me? What do you mean?"

"For your decision. For what happened today - before our wedding. Shortly after you and your family checked Nate out of the hospital, all I kept thinking about was you and how sad you were. How nobody paid attention to you."

Her eyes are starting to well.

"But I could see you," I continue. "And I knew God could. So I prayed. I prayed that He would reconcile you to Him and that you would finally have a close relationship - with Him."

She shakes her head. "All the questions that I had about Christianity. I thought I was just curious about your religion. Little did I know religion has nothing to do with it. Not when you're dealing with God."

I smile at her and kiss her forehead. She finally gets it.

Praise God.

"You still didn't answer my question," I point out. "Do you forgive them?"

She changes her position again and I bite back a groan. Maybe I'm not too tired after all. But I restrain myself as she lies back down against my chest, as if to hide from my probing eyes.

"I don't know. Sometimes I think I do. But then I realize that not thinking about people doesn't mean you've forgiven them. Sometimes I think I'm over it and then I'll see a paper with 'Jennifer Dawson' on it or 'Oliver Smith' and it all comes rushing back to me."

She looks so vulnerable, so haunted. I pull her close to me and kiss her forehead silently. I wait for her.

She speaks again. "I know that Christ calls us to forgive. I know that if He can forgive me, I can and have to forgive them. I just don't know how."

I nod and finally speak. "Forgiveness almost never starts with a feeling. It's a decision. To let it go and refuse to hold that trespass against that person. And you know what? You'll probably have to do it over and over and over again. But eventually…the feeling will follow the decision. It has to."

Two Weeks Later

Nicolette:

"Hmph!" The breath pushes out of me as I launch my foot in the air, striking the "X" on the punching bag with accurate precision. I glance up at the rafter holding the bag. Jason assured me that the beam was strong enough to withstand my drill when he installed it, but even after a year of using it, I still check and see. I'm in what used to be my house. When we're not busy honeymooning, Jason and I are busy moving all of my stuff into his house. Not one to waste time, my husband has already re-located the majority of my possessions into *our* new home. Not that he had a lot to move.

I think a part of me knew this is where we would end up so I never really made my house my home. I spent more time decorating and furnishing his place than I did mine because I knew it would be ours. My touches are all over the home we now share - but they've been there for over a year. One feature of this house that was uniquely mine was the punching bag. I take Krav Maga lessons every morning and train most afternoons on my own. I earned my Expert 4 black belt five weeks ago and in three week's time, hope to earn my Expert 5 level. Hence, the practicing, though I'd much rather train with my husband in an entirely different sport. Jason must have read my mind because I hear him calling me from our house a few yards over.

"Nic! Nic, hurry, get over here!"

I take a swig of water, swipe the back of my hand against my dripping forehead and jog over to our house. I pass the serene patio and join my husband in our living room. He's standing in front of the TV, eyes fixed on the screen. The fact that he's even watching it tells me something is up. We're not huge TV viewers. The channel is on CNN and I feel a tightening in my stomach. He glances at me and pulls me into his side, sweat and all.

"What's wrong?" I ask him. He shakes his head and nods at the screen.

"See for yourself."

I gasp at the headline. My name is in it.

"TALLOWAY BLOOD CAUSES GENETIC IMMUNITY."

As I try to wrap my head around what those words could possibly mean, Jason turns up the volume as the reporter, a blond woman in her thirties, continues.

"If you're just joining us on CNN this morning," I chuckle at the words. It's nearly seven in the evening here. "The breaking news of the hour is the recent discovery of what Nicolette Talloway's blood can do in the long term: an inheritance of genetic immunity."

I glance at Jason. His jaw is tight as the reporter speaks.

"Researchers at the Wakefield General Hospital Center for Hematology claim that the *children* of Talloway blood-recipients have a lifelong immunity to diseases if conceived and born *after* the parent has received the curative blood. Scientists claim that this immunity can be passed from either the father or mother. Refusing to hold a press conference, Dr. Montgomery Norris briefly stated to the press, 'Over the course of two years, since the initial clinical trials required volunteers to test the efficacy of Ms. Talloway's blood, those cured of their ailments went on to have children. These volunteers contacted the center at various stages, informing us of their children's perceived immunity to disease. When testing the blood of these children, we were able to confirm that their blood indeed functions very similarly to Ms. Talloway's. Their antibodies are next to invincible and do not succumb to the advances of antigens. Rather, they consume the invading bacteria or virus without any effort.'"

The screen cuts from Norris's statement to the reporter, who now turns to a panel of correspondents. I zone out during their introduction, my mind reeling from the information just disclosed. All this time, I just thought my blood could heal people. Never in a million years did I think it would affect those people's children and *their* immune systems. What does this mean for me? I glance at my husband once more. What does this mean for *us* and the life we've built here? I snap out of my thoughts as the panel starts their discussion.

The lead reporter opens. "Some really shocking news here. I don't think any of us could have anticipated the cure having such far-reaching consequences."

"How about 'benefits'?" a male panelist corrects. "This is remarkably good news. That not only can her blood cure cancer, it can prevent future generations from ever *having* cancer in the first place."

The panelist next to him nods her head in agreement, "Sam's right. If this blood can be distributed properly, there is a very real possibility that disease can be wiped off the face of the planet. Not that it would cease to exist but that we as a species would no longer be vulnerable to it. Can you even imagine such a world?"

There is a tinge of excitement at her words.

A different panelist, a young black woman, asks my question.

"What about distribution? So far, Nicolette Talloway has been the only known source of the cure. Do these children have her blood type now? Can their blood cure disease as well?"

Jason squeezes me closer to him. We listen closely for the answer.

The reporter looks down at her paper and shakes her head.

"No." My chest deflates at the word. "According to Dr. Norris, the head researcher at Wakefield, samples of the blood were tested against disease remotely and then administered to volunteers. For one thing, the blood of these children actually *have* specific types like A, B, AB, and O. If you recall correctly, Nicolette Talloway doesn't have a recorded blood type. Her blood is a universal donor and a universal recipient. When *her* blood is administered to others, it fights their disease or ailments. When the children's blood was administered to patients, it had the same effect of a regular blood transfusion but did not cure any ailments or disease. There is just enough of a genetic effect for their blood to fight domestic infections but nowhere near enough to combat others'."

The first panelist interjects, "I wonder what this would mean for these children's children. I mean, obviously, we won't know for years - the oldest child in this recent discovery just turned two - but it would be fascinating to see if the blood's effects carry on indefinitely or run out after several generations."

"One thing that is certain for now," the reporter replies. "Nicolette Talloway is still the only person whose blood can cure disease. And she's the only person whose blood can have this effect on future generations to come. And we have no idea where she is."

The reporter turns away from the panel and faces the camera alone. "In light of this recent discovery, questions have risen once more about the whereabouts of Nicolette Talloway."

My shoulder grows sore the more Jason squeezes me but I ignore it and tighten my arms around his waist.

A map appears on the screen with a pinpoint on San Diego, California.

"Talloway was last seen at the Sorona Detention Center in San Diego California over a year ago. It is believed that she escaped the facility with the help of Dr. Jason Monroe the night before she was scheduled to be transported to Washington D.C. Days after her escape, audio surfaced of her conversation with former President Brooklyn Carter, revealing Carter's direct role in the deaths of Talloway's parents, Thomas and Stacy Talloway. Impeached for obstruction of justice and perjury, Carter narrowly escaped removal from office by two votes and was forced to make reparations to the Talloway's two known surviving children, Natalia and Nathaniel. François Hollande's successor, President Antoine Sion, has promised to continue protecting Talloway's siblings under France's political asylum. Two months ago, the pair moved from Bordeaux to Paris upon Natalia's graduation from *Université Michel de Montaigne Bordeaux Trois*."

The lucky duck landed a job right out of college. She works as an anchor with a local Paris news station. Her fluent French came in handy after all.

The screen cuts footage of the new president, Bentley Lewis, walking across the White House lawn. He couldn't look more different than Brooklyn Carter. She was relatively young, in her late thirties, with auburn hair and an attractive enough face. Bentley Lewis looks as stodgy as they come. An old white man in his sixties with white hair and a medium build, which would be heavy if it weren't for his tall stature. Maybe he was handsome in his youth, maybe not. Either way, what he lacks in looks, he more than makes up for in power. The footage cuts to him sitting in the White House press parlor with a foreign diplomat by his side.

A reporter asks him, "Have you heard about the recent Talloway blood discovery and if so, what actions will the U.S. take to secure more of the cure?"

President Lewis shakes his head and quickly says, "While I am thrilled for the children who have this genetic immunity, and the parents who were fortunate enough to pass it down, the U.S. will not continue to pursue Nicolette Talloway for the use of her blood. She is welcome to return to her country without any fear of ramification in light of the atrocities of my predecessor, but we will not harass this young woman, regardless of what her blood can do."

A deep breath of relief leaves my lungs before I can even help it. I feel Jason's grip relax just the slightest at the man's words. We watch for a few more minutes before Jason turns it off. Slowly, he lets me go and walks into the kitchen while I sit on the couch and close my eyes. I hear him return a few moments later and open my eyes as he passes me a glass of water. I didn't realize how thirsty I was. I drink to my heart's content as he sits opposite me on the couch. We look at each other for a few minutes. I don't even care to process the new information about what my blood can do. I only care about him - about our life together.

"Do we have to move?" I ask him.

His eyes are thoughtful as he runs his fingers through his thick blond hair. He sighs.

"We probably should."

"I don't want to," I quickly reply.

"Neither do I but it might be more prudent to leave."

"Lewis said he wasn't going to pursue this."

"That doesn't mean other countries won't," he points out. "Besides, we don't know if Lewis means what he says. Remember all of the spins Carter gave to the press?"

How could I forget? The woman gave several bald face lies to the American people while she hunted me like it was open season. The thought of it sends chills down my spine. I shudder involuntarily and Jason strokes my leg in comfort. He reaches over to the phone on the coffee table beside us and makes a call. I watch him, curious enough to observe but not enough to ask.

"Hey, it's me." he says. "Are we safe?"

As soon as he asks, I know who he's called. He waits for a few moments, quickly thanks her, hangs up and smiles at me.

"What did she say?" I ask.

"She gives her regards as usual." He stretches and yawns. "We should be okay. She checked as many databases as she could but could see no planned or immediate action to find you."

"Can we stay?" I ask again. He looks at me for a long moment and slowly nods.

"For now. But we need a plan in case things change."

He means *go wrong*.

He stands up and walks to his desk in our bedroom. I follow him and for the next two hours, we do just that. Plan. Prepare. Hope for the best but expect the worse. And for the first time since marrying, we go to bed and do nothing but sleep. We're too drained for anything else.

About the Author

Michelle N. Onuorah is the bestselling author of *Type N, Remember Me, Double Identity*, and *Wanna Be on Top?* Originally from Maryland, Michelle grew up with a love of storytelling. She wrote down some of her stories in a notebook and continued to write for fun. At the tender age of thirteen, she wrote her first book, *Double Identity*, and got it published the next year. For three years, she ran an independent magazine, *MNO*, and served as the main writer and editor-in-chief. In 2009, Michelle won the *Captured Moments Creativity Award* for her poem entitled *Encounter*. Her writing has appeared in *Vestiges Literary Magazine, Avalon Literary Review*, and *Medium.com* among others. Michelle also enjoyed a successful career as a model in her teens, walking down runways during New York Fashion Week. In August of 2013, Michelle broke several of Amazon Kindle's Bestsellers lists for her debut novel, *Type N*. The following year, she enjoyed another bestseller with the well-loved novel, *Remember Me*. A graduate of Biola University, Michelle continues to write and publish under her company, MNO Media, LLC (www.mnomedia.com). You can learn more about Michelle at that website as well as like her page at www.facebook.com/authormichelleonuorah. Those interested in being notified of her new releases can go to www.tinyletter.com/mnomedia.

Check out these other titles by Michelle N. Onuorah:

Taking Names
Remember Me
Wanna Be on Top?

Order your copy today!